# THE
# BLUE
# TOWER

THREE CORD
PRESS

BOOK ONE OF THE FIVE TOWERS

# THE BLUE TOWER

a novel by

## J.B. SIMMONS

Copyright © 2018 by J.B. Simmons
All rights reserved
Cover by Jocker Benitez.

ISBN 978-1386556251

Published in the United States by Three Cord Press
www.threecordpress.com


www.jbsimmons.com

*The colors are acts of light; its active and passive modifications:*
*thus considered we may expect from them some explanation*
*respecting light itself.*

Johann Wolfgang von Goethe

.

# 1

THE FIRST THING I know: I'm treading water.

My legs and arms move by instinct, churning out circles of waves, like I'm a pebble dropped into a still lake. Beyond the ripples stretches a glassy surface into darkness. The air smells briny, with a hint of fish.

I swing my arms through the lukewarm water to turn. Behind me rises a wall as high as I can see. I take two strokes and reach it. I press my hands to the surface, my feet kicking to keep me afloat. My hands look pale and small as I push against the smooth, solid stone. It doesn't budge.

Panic grips me. Maybe the wall goes all the way around. I look up and see blackness. I peer down through the water. No bottom in sight. No creatures either. Must stay calm and breathe.

When I turn again there's a tiny dot of light that has appeared in the distance. Where did the light come from? How did I even learn to swim?

Doesn't matter. Survival, the cruel master, compels me forward. I push off the wall toward the light.

My body aches by the time I glimpse the shore. The light takes shape as a small blue orb by the water's edge. My strokes quicken. I'm breathing hard as my feet first touch the soft, muddy ground.

I crawl out of the water, then lay on my back, panting. Waves lap steadily at the shore. Beyond that there's a low rumble of moving air, like an ocean breeze in a cavern.

Then I hear a soft footstep. I open my eyes.

A hooded face gazes down at me. It is old and wrinkled and bearded, with black wire glasses that are barely wide enough to contain two blue eyes.

"Welcome, boy. I've been waiting a long time for you."

I rush to my feet and back away, splashing into the shallows. The man stands still.

"Who are you?" I ask, surprised by the young sound of my voice.

"I'm the leader of this tower." The blue light moves. It glows from the top of a staff in the old man's hand.

"What tower?"

"The Blue Tower. Dreadfully damp down here, don't you think?"

The man's gentle voice does not comfort me. The staff's light casts shadows like bruises over the sharp lines of his face. The light does not reach any walls. We're surrounded by darkness. My hands cover my face, pressing my temples, searching desperately for a memory.

The man steps closer and clasps my shoulder, his hand squeezing gently. The sleeve of his gray robe hangs down below his arm. His silver beard flows down to his waist.

"Give it time," he says.

I move to his side, keeping my distance. Surely I can outrun him if it comes to it. But then what? Another swim in the dark lake? I shiver at the thought of it.

"You're cold." He reaches into his robe and pulls out a folded cloth. He tosses it to me.

The fabric in my hands is plain but soft. I unfold it and discover a gray-blue robe. I'm wearing nothing. I slip on the robe.

"Good," he says. "We should go before the tide rises."

"There's a tide?"

"The sea rises and falls." He looks past me, into the dark cavern. "Like the towers. But maybe you'll change that. Blue is due to rise."

He begins walking away from the water. As I follow him, I realize how small I am. Maybe half his size. Something about it seems off. Either he's far too big, or I'm far too small.

"Where are we going?" I ask.

"This path is long," he says over his shoulder. "But the slope is gentle. It winds up the whole tower."

The ground changes from mud to stone. The stones are immense blocks, cool under my bare feet. The path reaches a wall, like the one that was behind me in the water. I feel like the wall has cut off my memories and everything I knew before. Questions are flooding into me and begin to spill out. "How did I get here?"

He pauses and glances back. "You followed someone."

"Who?"

He turns without answering and continues ahead. We follow the path along the wall, going up. The only light is the pale blue glow from the old man's staff. His robe swishes from side to side as he climbs.

*I followed someone?* I don't even remember anyone… It makes me feel very alone. It almost makes me glad that this old wizard found me. "If you won't tell me who I followed," I say, "at least tell me where we're going."

"Your room," he answers, without slowing. "You may rest there, have a bite to eat, before your first class."

"Class?"

He stoops down, his spectacled eyes level with mine. "Curiosity is good. Probably why you came to Blue first."

I return his stare. His eyes are bluer than the orb on his staff. Blue like the sky on a sunny day, not like this tower and its dark water and walls.

A hint of a smile appears under his beard. "You'll be okay here. There's a way out, unlike the other place you could have gone…" He breathes deeply. "But no looking back now, not yet. First food, then rest, then class. You'll need your energy for the Scouring."

"Scouring? What's that?"

"It's the only way out."

# 2

THE OLD WIZARD leads me past dozens of closed doors on the path up through the tower. Most are the same: plain slabs of wood that fit seamlessly into the immense stone wall. Other people must be here, but we do not see a soul. The quiet unnerves me. Maybe others are behind the doors, like this is some kind of prison. Or an asylum. Or worse.

With each turn upward I look for a window, hoping for some glimpse outside. But I see no windows, only the cold stone path circling up and up, coiling around the hollow core that now falls hundreds of feet below, to the place where I began. The hollowness pulls at me, taunting me, and there's no railing to interfere. The higher we go, the more I keep close to the wall, with my eyes on the ground. My legs feel heavy as lead when we finally stop before one of the doors.

"This is your room," the wizard says.

The door, like all the others, bears no number and is twice my height. I have no idea how the man knows this door is the right one. He pulls it open without knocking, and motions me inside.

I hesitate.

"You're tired," he says. "You will sleep here."

Past him there's a small, neat space enclosed in stone, about six paces across. Bed on one side. Desk, chair, and a small empty fireplace on the other. The furniture looks like worn, simple wood. Fresh salty air blows through a square opening in the wall.

*A window!* I glimpse water and sky outside. My spirits rise.

"You'll like the view," he says.

The fresh air lures me forward. I step through the door and stand in the middle of the room, breathing deeper.

"Kiyo will bring food soon." The man is still in the doorway, holding his staff like he's ready to cast some spell.

"Why am I here?" I ask.

"Get some rest." He ducks back through the door and starts to close it.

"Wait."

He pauses, eyes unreadable behind his glasses.

"Can't you tell me anything else?"

He taps his staff on the ground. The blue orb glows at the top of it. "I must go now." His voice is warm but firm. "Kiyo will come. She'll take care of you."

The door closes, leaving me alone in the room. I go to the door and find no handle. I push and it doesn't budge. I push harder. Still nothing. I kneel down and try to wedge my fingers underneath but can't.

Breathe. Don't panic.

Kiyo will come, whoever she is.

I move to the chair by the desk. A single drawer of the desk faces me. Inside there's a stack of paper, a small jar, and a feather. I set the paper and jar on the table, put the feather into the jar, and close the drawer. When I pull the feather out of the jar, a drop of black ink falls on the page. I press the tip of the feather down. Ink spreads into a blob that looks like an eye staring back at me. With careful strokes, I draw three circles around the eye.

I drop the feather back into the jar. I have nothing to write.

The room has a bed with a plain white sheet, and underneath there's a metal pan. I inspect the walls, every corner.

It's empty. Like my mind.

A rustle of fresh air draws me to the window. It's an open gap as tall as I am and as wide as my shoulders. The view reveals a spectrum of blues—the bottom half is midnight blue ocean, the middle above the horizon is azure, the top half is cloudy, gray-blue sky.

I reach my arms through the opening and just barely grasp the other edge. The stone wall is as thick as an oak. I pull myself up into the small space, squeezing through head first on my belly. The stone presses against my shoulders. Tight fit, but I manage to inch forward and stick my head out of the window.

A blast of salty wind rushes up into my face. The view down sends my head spinning. The tower's wall is perfectly smooth until it meets rough stones far below. Waves crash into the black rock, sending sprays of white into the sky. There's a small, protected cove with a wooden dock and a few boats tied to it, bobbing up and down in the waves. The jagged cliff shore stretches as far as I can see in both directions. A few shrubs and small trees cling to the coast. There's no other sign of life.

I twist onto my back to look up. More smooth stone goes up and up until the tower ends in a point in the sky. It's like a tube, thicker at the bottom and ten times as high as it is wide. It makes me feel small and still as I lay there, halfway up a tower, stuck between the sea and the sky.

The wind whips at my hair. I close my eyes.

*The Blue Tower*, the man said. Everything here is blue. My thoughts wind up and around the tower and drift into the cloudy sky above. I have no memories to root me down. I feel like a rain drop, evaporated and hovering listlessly in the clouds. I could float anywhere.

Something taps at my feet, making my body jerk reflexively. Eyes wide, I surge up and see a serene face watching me from my room.

It's a girl.

# 3

THE GIRL STANDS in the middle of my room, hands folded innocently in front of her. She looks about twelve years old. She's wearing a plain gray-blue robe like mine.

"Hi."

I climb down from the window and stand in front of her, straightening my robe. Her straight black hair and porcelain skin carry a stoic dignity. Her eyes are narrow and dark as night, with flecks of gold like stars. We're about the same height.

Past her, the door is closed. "I didn't hear you come in."

"It's the wind. Very loud this high up." She bows gracefully. "I'm Kiyo. What's your name?"

"I...don't know."

"What would you like to call yourself?" Her voice is small, a whisper compared to the roaring wind outside the tower.

It's an overwhelming question. I have no name. I need a name. I tuck my hands into the pockets of my robe, thinking. Many words come to me, and somehow I understand how my mind works, neurons firing in my cortex, but this means nothing without memories.

As the moments pass, Kiyo waits. She remains perfectly

still and silent. Her expression is impossible to decipher.

Then it hits me.

"Cipher," I say, testing the word. It fits, like a secret code to others, allowing them to unlock my attention. "You can call me Cipher."

"Nice to meet you, Cipher." She moves to the table, where a tray now sits beside the paper and ink jar. She lifts the cover off the tray, revealing a plate of steaming food. "Dinner's usually the same," she says. "Seaweed salad. Fish soup."

"Why?"

"I guess because that's what we have, being by the ocean. You get used to it. Helps you sleep."

"Who's *we*?"

"Us. Me. The leaders of the Blue Tower."

"That guy who looks like a wizard?"

She grins, sending a ripple of warmth into the cold and barren room. "His name's Abram. The other leader is Sarai."

"How long have you been here?"

"Many Scourings." Her gaze drops to her feet.

I shake my head, confused. "What's a Scouring?"

"It's like a battle between the towers. There are five of them. We use the Scourings to measure time."

"Oh." Now the revelations come too quickly. I don't know where to start with my questions. The room is quiet as we stare at each other, the two of us in this giant tower that apparently fights against other towers and feeds us seaweed. "Do you remember anything before you showed up here?"

She blinks at my question. Her eyes take on an eerie blankness. "Only a little. I've been to the Sieve…" Her last word comes out as a whisper.

"The Sieve?"

She backs toward the door. "You should eat, then sleep. Tomorrow will be a big day, your first class."

"What's the Sieve?" I step forward, not wanting her to leave.

She bows slightly. "I will see you tomorrow, Cipher."

"No, wait…"

The words are hardly out of my lips before she quickly opens the door and slips through.

I rush to the door, grabbing for it, but my hand pulls back at the last moment, instinct not letting me stick fingers into the inch-wide gap before it slams shut. The solid slab of wood does not budge when I shove it. I bang my fist on the door and shout for Kiyo.

There is no answer. The wind howls outside the window.

How did she open the door? It must be possible.

Trying not to panic again, I sit down at the table and stare at the food. Abram said Kiyo would come, and she did. Kiyo said there would be tomorrow, so maybe there will be.

The smell of the food convinces me to try a bite. The fish soup tastes good. The seaweed not so much. But I devour all of it, then slide the tray away.

The paper still sits on the table. The blob of ink with the three circles I drew around it looks up at me. My fingers rub along the feather's soft edge, then pull it from the jar. I write down seven words:

*Cipher*

*Kiyo*

*Abram*

*Scouring*
*Sieve*
*Blue Tower*

It's a start. I hold the quill ready above the paper, hoping some deep-down memory will come to me. My eyes close. What happened before I was treading water at the base of the tower? I know that people are born as babies to mothers. They don't suddenly appear in lakes. But I can't remember my mother, my father, or anything else. I put the feather back in the jar and move away from the desk.

The bed looks inviting. My head rests on the soft white fabric. My eyelids are heavy. As the sound of the ocean lulls me to sleep, the words Scouring and Sieve tumble over and over in my mind like grains of sand in the waves.

# 4

THE SMELL OF bread and brine wakes me. I sit up in bed, the ocean air pulling goosebumps out of my skin. A small loaf and cup are on the table. The door is closed, no one in sight. The bumps along my skin rise higher. Someone has been in the room.

I feel like I've slept for days. At least I remember waking up in the water, in the dark. The wizard, Abram, brought me to this room, and Kiyo brought me food. Still I remember nothing from before the tower.

My stomach rumbles. I try the bread, and it's not bad. A bit stale, a bit cool. I wash it down with the water. I'm chewing my last bite when the door opens.

It's Kiyo. She enters smoothly, with her hands folded in front of her just like yesterday. "Good morning, Cipher."

I motion to the empty plate. "Did you bring the food?"

She shakes her head no. "Ready?"

"Yes." I'm already moving to the door. No way she's leaving again without me. But of course the door doesn't budge when I push it.

Kiyo looks amused. "I felt the same way."

I study her as she turns to the closed door. She presses

her hand to a stone beside it. Nothing moves. Her hand is still, her face concentrated. Then there's a click.

The door swings open.

I quickly step outside. A wooden bar has lifted on the other side. I turn back to Kiyo. "How'd you do that?"

A faint color of pink touches her porcelain cheeks. "I lifted the bar."

"How?"

"With my mind."

"Seriously?" I study her carefully. She's not smiling, not joking. "Is it magic?"

"If you want to learn, you'll come with me." She steps past me and starts walking up the path through the tower. The only other way to go is down, past closed doors and to the dark lake below.

So I follow her, watching her small pale feet on the huge dark stones. I figure I must have died, and that's how I got here. But I'm not sure. Seems like I would remember if I'd died. It's supposed to hurt, right? And anyway, my heart is still pumping, my brain thinking, and my legs moving. I certainly feel alive.

We pass dozens of closed doors, not a soul in sight. The spiraling path grows narrower as we go up through the tower, winding like a hollow helix and drawing so close that I could almost jump across from one side to the other. But the bottom is far enough down to make me hug the wall.

"Why isn't anyone else here?" I ask.

"Everyone's busy."

She stops in front of a door. It's plain wood like the others. She presses her hand to it, then meets my eyes.

"Easier to listen at first, okay?"

I say okay, but I'm thinking about her eyes. They are dark and innocent, yet look like they've seen many things. She told me before that she went to the Sieve and remembers a little. What did she see?

She opens the door and leads the way in.

I move to follow but stop, stunned by the space in front of me. It's not a room. It's a palace hall. White marble floors with bluish veins spread before me a hundred feet. There are others here, sitting in desks like students. They are dwarfed by the thick columns, which hold up an arched ceiling so high I can't make out the seams between the stones. The far wall is all glass.

I expect to see ocean beyond, but instead there are four spires rising high in the sky. They are majestic, in entirely different ways: closest to the left is a castle glimmering like yellow crystal, beside it is an immense green tree with intricate ropes and wooden platforms scattered through its branches, then a red keep rising from a rocky peak, and last, closest to the right, is a round black tower that looks like an iron pole. The towers are close together, surrounding a paved space enclosed in a high wall. The land beyond each of the other towers extends as far as I can see. The yellow castle has golden fields beyond it. The towering green tree has a vast forest. Red has ranges and ranges of mountains. Black has hills with rows and rows of flooded terraces that glisten darkly under the slate sky.

"Welcome, Kiyo." A woman is walking towards us. A dozen faces are turned, staring at me. "Who have you brought?"

"His name is Cipher," Kiyo says.

The woman stops in front of me. She is almost as tall as Abram. She leans forward like a wave about to crash. Her skin and eyes are as dark as onyx. There are streaks of gray at the edges of her black hair. Her gaze seems a little lost, a little sad. Her long hands find my cheeks. It feels like a splash of cold water. "Nice to meet you, Cipher. I am Sarai. Abram tells me you have many questions. This is natural and good. We must rebuild what is missing inside us, yes?"

My voice comes out faintly: "I would like that."

The woman stands up straight, and her long hands clasp together. "Very good. Come, both of you. I was just telling the class about the final stone of our tower."

Kiyo and I follow her through the great hall. Our bare feet make the softest sound against the marble, but the room is so silent that even our quiet footsteps echo. The faces watching us are normal, other boys and girls. They wear faded robes like ours. Their expressions are filled with wonder.

No one says a word as Kiyo takes her seat. She points to an empty desk beside hers. The smooth wood looks as if it has been worn down by a million students. I take the spot, the last empty one in the room.

Sarai suddenly claps. "Good news, class." We all look at her, but she's looking straight at me. "At long last, we have our final student, *and* our wind. It's time to sail."

# 5

THE TEACHER, SARAI, stands before our group of students, with the glass wall behind her showcasing the four towers in the distance. I count twelve students in the room. Six boys, six girls.

"Our land of five towers is older than any memories," Sarai explains. "The towers were made by the same word that made earth. The towers have a similar purpose for us, but it will be revealed only in the fullness of time, because we remain connected with our former home." Sarai's hands draw large circles in the air, the sleeve of her robe trying to catch up with the movements. Maybe Abram really is a wizard, she's a sorceress, and we're all under a spell.

"Here, in Blue, we have water in abundance," she says. "It brings many gifts to sustain us. And we look into the water of the Sieve to see what we must see. Because we all must understand what has been done before we can undo it. Not that we can undo the past, but we can wash away the stains that it has left on each of us."

She pauses, studying us. I don't know what to think of her words, but I need to find this Sieve. Maybe Kiyo will tell me more about it.

A boy sitting in the front raises his hand. "Why do we see things in the Sieve?"

Sarai's eyes are ablaze with energy. "I do not answer why."

"Well...when did...the things we saw, when did they happen?" the boy asks.

"Before you came here," she answers.

Another student raises her hand, the sleeve of her robe sliding down her skinny arm. "If water is supposed to wash us clean, is the same thing happening in the other towers?"

Sarai swirls toward the student, swaying slightly as she speaks. "Only *we* are of the sea. Each tower has its own way, its own purpose."

"Is it fire for the Red Tower?" The girl's voice sounds small.

"Yes. And what quenches fire?"

I gaze out the glass wall at the four spires. The mountainous red one has a flame rising out of it like a torch. The other towers have their own colors. Green, Black, and Yellow. They must have people inside—maybe boys and girls staring out at our Blue Tower, back at me.

"Water," a boy answers.

"Water," Sarai agrees, "is always the strongest. But victory is not assured. What is our greatest weakness?"

"We freeze when it's cold?" answers the same boy, and a few of the students laugh.

"This is a danger," Sarai says, "but the temperature is not a threat during the Scouring. Only the other towers are."

No one speaks. An odd silence falls over the room, and I can't help but ask, "What is the Scouring?"

Every face in the room turns to me. Sarai approaches my desk, plants her hands on the two sides, and leans close. "Do you know why you are here?"

I shake my head.

Sarai smiles widely. Her teeth are perfectly white, perfectly straight. "You know the definition of Scouring. That's what it is."

She's right. I remember the definition. *Scour: to remove the dirt from something by rubbing it hard with something rough.* And scouring is the process of this removal. But that hardly answers my question.

"It removes dirt?" I ask. "What dirt?"

"That's for Abram to show you. In this class we're focused on the scrubbing, not the dirt." She steps back and glances around the room. "Would any of you like to tell Cipher what you have learned about the Scouring?"

The others look afraid. One boy raises his hand confidently.

"Max?" Sarai says.

"It's the fight between the towers," he answers. "Each tower sends out a team of twelve. The teams try to capture boys and girls from each other and bring them back to their own tower."

"Close enough," Sarai says. "It will continue until there is balance among the towers, and until the impure are scoured." She glances at me. "Maybe purity is coming, now that our numbers are complete. So…I was asking, what is Blue's greatest weakness?"

Quiet again.

Kiyo raises her hand. "If you separate water, each drop

becomes small and vulnerable."

"Precisely. We have power only when we're united." Sarai glides to the front of the room. She motions to a small table there, where a piece of white paper sits. "Your assignment is here."

She pulls something out of her robe and sets it on the table. It's an hourglass, with sand falling slowly from the top bulb to the bottom. "Stay at your desks until the time passes," she says. "If one of you gets the paper before then, you may leave for lunch."

She slips away from the desk to the wall of glass. She leans back on it, watching us.

"How are we supposed to get it?" one of the students asks.

"Sarai won't tell us," Max says. He has straight black hair and looks like he might be from the same kind of place as Kiyo. Except he's not like Kiyo. She's delicate and elegant, but he looks fierce, with a wide jaw and hard, narrow eyes. "It's the same every time," he says. "We just have to sit here until the stupid sand is done." He leans his head down on his desk as if taking a nap.

"What are you doing?" asks a girl. She is watching Kiyo, who holds out her arms toward the desk, straining like she's trying to lift something.

Kiyo's arms fall. "I'm trying to pick up the letter."

"Kiyo thinks she's a magician," Max mumbles, his head still down. A few others in the class laugh.

Kiyo lifts her arms again defiantly, this time pointing at Max.

More of the students are laughing at her.

"Crazy Kiyo," someone says.

But Max jerks his head off the table, glaring at Kiyo. "What are you doing?"

She smiles and folds her arms on the desk. "Oh, you felt that?"

"No," he barks, then glances around the room. "Crazy Kiyo…"

"I know you felt it," Kiyo says, but she does not sound sure. "The teacher wouldn't tell us we can get the paper unless there's some way to do it."

Sarai is still by the window, gazing outside as if ignoring us.

"Tiny Kiyo the sorceress," Max says. "You've got no chance in the Scouring. Some boy from Red would steal you if you were good for anything."

The girl beside Max giggles. She has curly auburn hair and a round, pretty face. "I hope a boy from the Green tower steals me," she says.

Max grins. "We know, Helena. They'll take you before Kiyo, that's for sure."

Kiyo's face has flushed red. Her lower lip quivers, and she puts her head down.

"We should use Kiyo as bait," Max says.

My jaw clenches. This isn't right. Kiyo hasn't done anything wrong. She doesn't deserve this. I feel…angry.

I stare down Max. "Don't talk to her like that."

Max's sneer swivels to me. "So, the newbie is Kiyo's defender? The valiant class runt!"

More laughter, louder.

"He's so little." Helena catches my eyes. "You're cute.

How old are you, nine?"

"Cipher and Kiyo," Max says. "The love birds!"

Kiyo hides her face, head down on the desk. Time slows and everything but Max fades away. A huge wave of anger surges up through my core and into my arms. It makes my fists shake. It tingles into my fingers. I raise them and point them at Max's throat. The anger channels through my arms and fingertips, to hurl, to squeeze.

Wind suddenly whips past me.

It slams into Max like a fist, blowing him back, flipping him over his desk, sending him sliding across the floor. He stops with a thud against the glass wall, near the teacher's feet.

Time returns to normal speed. I hear shouting. All eyes are on me.

# 6

I'M THE ONLY student standing, and the other students gape at me in shock. Somehow the wind came from me. It blew Max thirty feet across the room. I'm terrified of what I did, but a little proud. He deserved it.

My arms fall to my sides, and Sarai is there.

"Cipher, Cipher," she is saying.

Her eyes are deep pools. My breathing slows.

"You must learn to control this," Sarai says, a hint of a smile in her eyes. "I asked you to get the paper, not to blow another student across the room."

She turns to face the others, her back to me, protecting me. "We must stay united. Our power must be used against the others in the Scouring. So why do you provoke each other?"

No one responds. Max is hugging his knees, on the far side of the room.

Sarai walks to the small table at the front of the room where she had left the piece of paper. She kneels down and picks up the paper from the floor. Maybe the wind blew it off the table. Maybe I did it.

Sarai returns and hands me the paper. It's an envelope.

"Lead them to lunch," she says. "Read it there."

The envelope weighs down my arm like an anvil in my hand. The other kids stare at it, or at me, looking scared.

Kiyo comes to my side. She doesn't look scared. "I'll show you the way."

She takes my hand and guides me out of the hall. The rest of the class follows, murmuring behind us.

"Thank you," Kiyo whispers, "for what you did. I've been wanting to do that for a long time."

We descend through the tower on the spiral pathway. Kiyo and I walk in the front. Max stays at the back of our group. Whenever I glance at him, he looks away. One day into this place and already I have an enemy.

While we're walking I try moving the air again. I look down at the envelope and concentrate on making wind blow at it, just to shake it a little. I visualize it blowing out of my hand and whirling to the floor.

Nothing happens.

Was it my anger that did it before? I don't have anything against the envelope, not like I had against Max. Trying to feel angry again doesn't work. But Sarai said I could learn to control this...

The air starts to grow damper, like we're underground. I figure we're near the bottom of the tower, near the cavern where I appeared, treading water, without a single memory.

"How much farther?" I ask Kiyo.

"We're close. You should lead the way in, like Sarai said."

"Then what?"

"Just go in and find an empty table for us." Kiyo glances back at the others. They're watching us, listening to every

24

word. "Make sure the table fits twelve."

Kiyo stops us in front of a huge set of open doors. They were not open when I passed them before. She nods ahead, and I lead the way through.

As I step inside, my feet freeze in place. The room is even more spectacular than the classroom far above. The walls are crystal clear glass, as are the floor and ceiling.

We're completely underwater.

# 7

"A TABLE," KIYO says, nudging me forward.

I step from the stone pathway and onto the glass—toes first, gently. The clear floor doesn't budge, even as I see a jellyfish floating under my feet. I move into the room, pulling my eyes away from the aquatic life below to find an empty table.

The tables in the room are thick round slabs of dark wood, each with a candle burning in the center. Some tables are empty. The full ones have about twelve kids sitting around them. I remember what Max had said about the Scouring. *Twelve from each tower.*

But there are dozens of kids in this room. How do they choose which twelve go to the Scouring? Everyone is young, but some look a little older than our group. Their robes are different, too. Several are royal blue with three white satin stripes on the sleeves. A few are midnight blue with four stripes. Scattered throughout the room are boys and girls wearing plain white robes and carrying trays of food. Some wear silver bands around their necks, some don't.

A boy catches my eyes as I pass his table. His long brown hair hangs down over the shadow of a beard. His dark blue robe has four white stripes.

"Lost?" he says in a low voice. "Second class is back there." He points to an empty table at the far side of the room.

"Thanks," I say, moving ahead and wondering what it means to be second class.

As we approach the empty table, wedged into the corner between two walls of glass, I notice that I'm not alone in my fascination with the view. Everyone in my class gazes through the glass as a school of silvery fish sweep past us. A darker, larger form darts after them, splitting the school into two parallel arcs. A shark chasing minnows.

The water's surface is far above. We must be fifty feet down. It would almost be too dim to see if not for the candles on each table. The blend of obscure light from above and candles within gives the whole room a dreamlike glow.

Kiyo takes the seat beside me. Her pale face has a bluish hue, reflecting the water around us.

"How did they make this room?" I ask her.

"Sarai says a wave carved it out."

"Some wave." I look out over the other tables. There are almost a hundred others in here. "Do you know anyone in the other groups?"

"A few," Kiyo says.

"I know lots of them," says the girl sitting beside Kiyo. She's the one who laughed with Max, mocking Kiyo and me. She's also stunning, with almond eyes and long curls falling like waves down her back. "I started with another group. My name is Helena, by the way."

"How'd you change groups?" a friendly-looking boy asks.

He's sitting to my other side. He's a lot bigger than I am.

"It was after my last trip to the Sieve," Helena says. She's leaning forward, something conspiratorial about it. I notice the others huddling closer now, too. But no one else in the room seems to pay us any attention.

"What'd you see?" the boy asks.

She gives him a stony look. "You know the rules, Hank."

"Come on. Just tell us a little?"

"Okay…" Helena takes a deep breath. "I saw a woman serving drinks in a crowded inn. The woman was beautiful, with long curly hair like mine. It might have been me."

"It was," Hank says. "It always is."

"I guess so. And I hope so." Helena smiles. "Because she was serving a royal delegation staying a night at her inn. She even served the emperor. The soldiers there called him Constantius. He was everything you would expect an emperor to be, with a golden olive branch on his head and a purple robe down his back. He brought his own golden chalice that I—this woman, I mean—used to serve him the finest wine at the inn. He seemed to notice the woman more as the night wore on, and the candles burned low. It was late when he finally spoke to her, placing his hand gently over her wrist after she filled his chalice again. *Your bracelet,* he said, *where did you get it?* The woman looked down, and I saw that she wore a silver bracelet, with hammered metal and a cross at the clasp. *My father,* the woman said. *He gave it to me as a gift when I was young.* The emperor held up his wrist beside hers. He wore a bracelet that looked exactly the same. *Mine was a gift from my mother,* he said, smiling as he looked into the woman's eyes. *Will you join me tonight, and when we go?* The woman did not hesitate. She agreed to go."

Helena stops and looks around the table, as if remembering where she is. "That was it. Then I was out of the Sieve. So I go to sleep and this morning I'm assigned to you guys. It's good to be back with some of you. Second class!"

"Nice work," Hank says. "It took me forever to get promoted from first class. We're not all geniuses here. I bet I gutted a thousand fish, delivered a thousand trays…"

"What's first class?" I ask, wondering as I look at the others' faces if every one of them has seen the past. "Are we supposed to learn something in the Sieve before we get to second class?"

No one answers. Eleven sets of eyes are staring at me.

"What?" I ask.

"No one just starts in second class," Helena says. "And no one does what you did with the wind. Who are you?"

"I'm Cipher. And…that's about all I know."

Helena does not look satisfied with my answer. "How did you make the wind blow like that?"

"I just got angry." I glance at Max sitting on the opposite side of the table, scowling.

"Maybe emotion is the key," Kiyo says. "Sarai teaches that we all can do it."

Hank is shaking is head, looking at me. "It can't be that simple. You're the first I've seen who actually pulled it off, much less moved something big."

I don't know how to respond.

"Fourth class can do it," Helena says.

"Blow a person all the way across the room?" Hank

replies, brow raised.

"Well…" Helena grins at me. "Maybe wonder boy got lucky."

Others around the table start whispering among themselves.

Hank puts his arm around my shoulder. "Don't worry about them," he says. "They're just jealous."

"Thanks," I say, not exactly comforted. "So what's first class?"

He explains it to me, with Kiyo chiming in. They say that when people first arrive in the Blue Tower they have to do grunt work like preparing food or cleaning. Kids in higher classes supervise the work. If you do it for long enough without complaining, then Abram comes and takes you to the Sieve. I start to ask about that, but Hank clams up like Kiyo did. "That's a question for Abram," he says. "While you're at it, you may as well ask him why you skipped first class."

Two boys in white robes come to our table. They place steaming bowls in front of us. Smells like some kind of fish, but there's a tentacle hanging out of my bowl. Octopus? Squid?

I sip the broth. Not bad. I bite off a piece of the tentacle. Slimy, chewy, but it tastes okay.

We all inhale the food. I wonder what time it is. No way to tell. I remember what clocks are, but don't remember ever seeing one. I'm just eating this squid stew because that's what my body tells me to do.

Hank is watching me. His bowl is empty.

"What?" I ask.

"Are you going to open the note?"

I had forgotten. I retrieve the note from my robe and slide my thumb under the seal. I pull out the small note inside, but I can't read it. There are a bunch of symbols I don't understand.

"Can anyone read this?" I ask, holding it out.

Kiyo takes it, studies it, and says no. Same for the next boy, and the next. The note stops at Max. His eyes open wide. He stares at it for a while, then looks around at us. I'm not sure if he's terrified or furious.

"It's a message from Abram."

# 8

MAX HOLDS THE envelope like it's a crab trying to pinch him. Most of the other kids in the underwater room have cleared out. It's eerily quiet for a moment, as a sea turtle glides by a few feet away.

"Go on," Helena says. "Read it."

"It's just a few words." Max turns the note around so we can all see the odd symbols on it. "Can anyone else understand it?"

No one else speaks up. I rack my brain for how this is possible. The writing must be a different language, but we all use the same language to talk with each other.

"How can you read it?" I ask.

Max glares at me. "Newbie wants my story. Didn't you hear Helena? We aren't supposed to share that stuff from the Sieve. No chance I'm telling you."

"I don't really care." It comes out harsher than I'd meant it. "I just want to know how you can read it. Is it a different language?"

"Newbie's feeling lost." Max laughs.

I start to feel angry again. He seems to have forgotten that I blew him out of his desk. My hand raises off the table.

"That's enough, both of you," Hank says firmly, and my hand lowers. He looks to me. "It is a different language. When Abram lets you look in the Sieve, you'll begin to learn from your past. Don't get too excited though. You probably won't like what you see." He turns to Max. "Can you read the note now?"

"It's instructions," Max says, studying the note again. "It reads: Cipher will lead you into the Scouring in two days. Your objective is to return safely to the Blue Tower with Emma."

Helena snatches the note away from Max. "The Scouring already? Who's Emma?"

Max's arms fall to his sides, like he's glad he doesn't have to hold the paper anymore. "It says Yellow after her name," he says. "That's all."

"How do we get ready for the Scouring?" I ask.

"Besides what you heard in class," Kiyo says, "about the fight between the towers, and trying to capture people from the other colors, none of us really know." She glances around the table. "None of us have been out of the tower yet, right?"

No one volunteers.

"It's the main reason we're here," says a girl with long red hair and a sad face. She had introduced herself as Mabel. "Abram told me we have to survive the Scouring to move on."

"Move on to where?" Max asks, still eyeing the note in Helena's hands. "This has to be a stupid game."

"Don't say that," Kiyo says softly.

"Why not?" Max stands, fists planted on the table. "We have no reason to trust Abram, or anybody else here."

Kiyo doesn't answer.

The red haired girl, Mabel, speaks up. "None of us remember anything before Abram let us see in the Sieve. He welcomed us, brought us in. Why *shouldn't* we trust him?"

"Seriously?" Max scoffs. "Abram probably kidnapped us, wiped our memories, and uses the Sieve to control us. He gave us this stupid assignment." Max points at me. "He's the one who put this wind-blower in charge of our group, even though he's the newbie. None of it makes sense. I'm not trusting anyone."

Helena places her hand on Max's arm, like a mother calming a petulant child. "But what about the Scouring?" she asks. "I don't think we have a choice. If Abram makes us go there, what else are we supposed to do?"

Max steps back from the table. "I say we fend for ourselves."

Hank stands up, facing Max. "The note says we follow Cipher. We all heard Sarai. We have to stay together."

"Suit yourself," Max says. "I'm leaving."

"But you can't—" Hank begins.

"Why not?" Max snaps. "You can't stop me."

Hank looks to me, as if seeking support. Despite his size, there's something timid about his soft face and sandy hair. I think he's right. Why not trust Abram? For good or bad, it seems like he's the only one who can show me the Sieve and my memories. Maybe he's the only one who can help us get out of here.

I nod at Hank.

"Idiots." Max turns to go. "Good luck out there."

Hank grabs Max's shoulder. "No. Sarai said to stay

together."

Max jerks away. "Let me go."

Hank grabs for him again, and Max swings. The punch lands square in Hank's face, but he hardly budges. He rears back his fist and goes at Max with a roundhouse.

Max ducks, then throws another punch. This time Hank staggers back, trips over a chair and goes down hard. I hear the heavy thud of his head on the glass floor.

Mabel and Kiyo rush to him. He's not moving. They shout for help.

Max flees the room. Helena follows after him.

I watch in a daze as two white-robed boys hurry in with a cart and take Hank away. The way they move, and how fast they came, makes me think this is not unusual. A fragment of a memory comes to me about people getting hurt. A word flashes in my mind: *hospital.* The word feels overwhelmingly familiar, but it's like a hollow jar with the meaning sucked out of it. The gap in my mind makes me dizzy, forcing me to my knees. My hands press on the clear glass as I stare into the water's dark depths below.

# 9

"WHO'S ON DISH DUTY?"

I look up from the glass floor, and the ocean creatures below, to see two new girls standing by our group's table. One of them is older, with three bands of white around the arms of her blue robe. The younger one wears a white robe and a silver band around her neck. She has wild brown hair.

"I am," Kiyo says. "And Cipher can help."

"Good. Let's go."

The older girl leads us away without glancing back. She must assume we'll obey, and her air of authority works. We follow her out the doors of the glass-enclosed dining hall, down the path a short distance, and into the next door. As we step in, a fishy smell wafts over us. Half-rotten fishy. It makes me gag.

"You two start washing," the girl says, looking at Kiyo and me. "Adele will dry and shelve."

Kiyo tugs on my sleeve to lead me away, but I can't resist a few questions. This girl seems to know what's going on. "Why is Adele wearing a white robe?"

The girl eyes me up and down. She has a strong frame and fists on her hips. She'd probably knock me to the floor if she tried, not that I'd fight her. "Cipher, right? I heard about what you did. How'd you get so much wind at once?"

"Um, I'm not sure." Word must have spread fast. "I guess I just got angry."

"You controlled your anger?"

"I think so."

"What did it feel like to have that much air under your control?"

She seems desperate to know. I don't really have any answers, but that doesn't stop me from grabbing some leverage. "I'll tell you," I say, "if you tell me why Adele is wearing a white robe...and that weird necklace band."

The girl gives me an amused smirk. "You've got guts, talking to me like that. I can see why Abram let you skip first class. But fine, it's a deal. By the way, I'm Shelley." She holds out her hand, and we shake.

"Nice to meet you."

"Likewise, newbie." She turns to Adele, the girl in white with the wild brown hair. "I captured Adele in the Scouring. She's from Green. Once you get your first capture, you're promoted to third class and whoever you capture becomes your servant."

"And the necklace?"

"It's called a link. That's how you keep your servant under control."

*A servant...under control?* Doesn't seem right. Adele's eyes are full of restless energy. There's a definite wildness about her. The link on her neck is not connected to anything.

"How does it work?" I ask.

"Blue Tower magic," the girl says. "It makes her do

whatever I want. In return, it makes me feel whatever she feels. I guess whoever made the links set them up that way to keep us from misusing it."

"Why doesn't she just take it off?"

"She can't. It makes her really sick if she tries. Lots of vomit."

"Oh."

"Don't feel too bad for her," Shelley says. "She always has a choice to join us. The Blue Tower initiation is supposed to be hard, but plenty have done it. I think Adele has a long way to go." The two girls exchange an odd look. "She really doesn't like us," Shelley says. "She feels...bored and disgusted with us."

"What happens if she joins Blue?"

"If she converts, the link comes off and she goes straight to first class, memories intact. If she refuses after a set period of time, she starts just like all of us did, with her mind wiped clean in the cavern below."

"Wait, all of us?" I blurt out. "You mean...did that happen to me?"

Shelley shakes her head. "Doubt it. I would recognize you."

"How long have you been here?"

"Long enough to make third class. Now I just need Adele to convert." Shelley looks to her servant. "Then you can work your way up. We're a meritocracy, after all. The best always rise. You could be strong."

Adele doesn't respond.

"Does it help you if she converts?" I ask Shelley.

"Oh yes. I've already survived two Scourings, so if she

converts, I'd make *fourth* class." She says this like it is the greatest thing in the universe.

"How many have made fourth class?"

"Not many. Now, I've answered your questions, newbie. Tell me how it felt to hold that much power?"

"It felt...terrifying."

"Anything else?"

"It only happened once."

"Think."

"It was so unexpected. I guess it felt like being in the eye of a huge storm, and knowing that wherever you go, the eye will move with you."

"I like that!" Shelley sighs. "But it doesn't teach me anything. If you think of more to tell me, maybe I'll let you off dish duty. Until then, you've got work to do." She points to a stack of dirty dishes on the far wall.

"What about Adele?" I ask. "Can't you make her do it?"

"It's your job, newbie." Shelley's hand rests on her hip. "Complain about it again and I won't even let Adele help you with drying. Better get started."

Kiyo has been listening quietly to all this, not saying a word. Now she gives me instructions about the cleaning. We stand before a sink as wide as I am tall. To the left are the dirty dishes. Dozens of bowls with the remains of squid soup. Kiyo gives me the job of dipping them into the water and giving them a first scrub, then she will polish off any final bits and pass it on to Adele to dry. Simple enough.

The work goes smoothly but slowly. My hands feel the effort. They're pruned and scalding in the water. I try to distract myself by counting the bowls as I go. Fifteen, sixteen…thirty…

The monotonous work starts to make me angry. What is the point of all this? As soon as I feel the emotion, I remember using the wind, and I decide to try again. My vision narrows on a single soapy bubble on a dirty bowl. I funnel all the anger and frustration and unanswered questions into a thread that I weave through my mind and toward the bubble. A wisp of air shakes the bubble slightly.

It's working.

I push harder and harder until the soap blows away. Then I form the air into a net that I use to lift the bowl while I scrub it. Next I move the net of air, holding the bowl, so that it drifts silently over to Kiyo.

She looks up from her scrubbing, surprised. "You're controlling it!"

I nod, smiling.

She grins back. "And you don't even look angry."

I continue practicing, shaping the air into circles and squares and webs. The largest shapes I can make are about the size of my fist. They blast little gusts at the dishes. It's getting fun. One batch of bubbles slips away and smatters Kiyo's cheek. We laugh together.

By the time we finally finish washing, I've counted 67 bowls total. That means 67 people ate lunch. The tower seems like it could hold many more than that.

Abram's words in the cavern come to me, *Blue is due to rise.*

# 10

IN THE AFTERNOON, our group of twelve gathers again with Sarai. Everyone is there, even Max. He sits on the opposite side of the room from Hank, who now wears a bandage around his head. Max keeps his eyes down, staring at his thumbs twiddling on the desk.

Sarai teaches us more about the other towers. She explains that Yellow and Green are our natural allies. Black and Red are our usual enemies. But it's not so simple, she says, because every group has an assignment during the Scouring. The assignments are a starting point, but the fight rarely goes as planned.

"Come, watch," she says. "That's the best way to learn."

We rise quietly and join her by the wall of glass. Our group seems to be in a somber mood, probably because of what happened with Max and Hank.

The view from this high takes my breath away. The surrounding lands stretch as far as I can see, but the other four towers are close—the black iron pole, the red mountain keep, the green tree, and the yellow castle. The towers look the same height, spaced about as far from each other as they are tall. In the center of the towers is a vast open space surrounded by a high gray wall with five sides—shaped like a pentagon. The gray ground of the open space is perfectly flat and empty. In the center of the pentagon there is a small white circle. There are gateways into the pentagon from each side, one for each tower. Our tower's gateway must be below us.

Sarai comes to my side. "You understand your assignment?"

"We're supposed to capture Emma from Yellow," I say, "and bring her back. But who's Emma?"

"You'll have to find her, without letting yourself get caught. Be constantly on your guard. And work together." She glances at Max. "We'll keep refining your group until you're ready."

"What happens if we can't find Emma, or capture her?"

"Then you start over," Sarai says, "as you will again and again, as many times as it takes."

That doesn't sound good. It seems too harsh. "You mean in the cavern, with my mind wiped?"

"Yes. Reset." She turns to the wall of glass. "Look, today's Scouring begins. You will see."

The gateways of each tower are opening below. Figures appear in them, their colors vivid against the gray wall and ground. A group from the Red Tower charges out. The twelve of them look as small as ants from our height. They fan out in pairs, going different directions. A group from Black is packed closely together. I can't count their number they're so close, but it's probably twelve. They march steadily forward like a solid cube of metal sliding across the open expanse. Groups from Green and Yellow move more slowly.

Those from Yellow form into a circle. Green takes an odd shape, like a snake slithering out from the gateway toward the middle. And the twelve from Blue, directly below us, makes sixty total out there.

Someone from Red reaches the center of the open ground. The person steps onto the white circle, which looks like quartz in the middle of the slate gray plaza. The red figure stops, in the middle of the white. The other colors continue approaching.

The phalanx of black figures gets there first. They slam into the red person, quickly overwhelming and covering the white stone. The other groups begin to surround the group from Black, as if testing it. The tip of the line of Green strikes at one edge of Black, while a few from the Blue Tower hover near the other edge. Yellow arcs out around a corner of the Black. The pairs from Red are dispersed everywhere, charging and bouncing through the other colors like pinballs.

The movements become too fast and scattered to follow. The colors—the people—are colliding, blending, in a sea of conflict. My eyes are drawn to a single boy from Blue. He's below us, close to our tower. He has long brown hair and stands beside a girl in a red dress. A boy from Red, with a helmet and beard and gleaming weapon, races toward them. Then, just as the Red attacker comes close, he's pushed back. He stays on his feet and comes again. He's flung back again.

"It's Stephen," Kiyo says beside me, with awe in her voice. "He's fourth class. He might capture one!"

The two fighters have not touched. Stephen must be using the wind like I did, maybe holding the girl from Red in place. But the boy from Red is relentless. This time he slows but is not flung back. He presses closer and closer until he collides with Stephen, who falls motionless on the ground. The pair from Red leave him there, charging off in a different direction.

"No..." Kiyo whispers.

My gaze returns to the center, stunned. Motionless figures now litter the open ground, and the battle rages on near the center. The block of Black fighters has broken, and it is impossible to identify any pattern in the colors. It is chaos. My body is tense, watching as moments pass and the fight continues.

Then everyone freezes in place.

A classmate beside me whispers, "Cover your eyes."

I turn and see Hank, blocking his eyes with his hands. Others are doing the same. I start to ask why when the flash comes.

Pure, blinding white.

Like a supernova explosion.

I blink furiously, trying to get my eyes back into focus. The blazing light floods my vision, like I've been staring at the sun.

When my eyes finally start to adjust, I see a giant pillar of light stretching from the white center of the fighting ground to the sky above. I can't see its top or make out its edges—it is like a spotlight beam shining up, but made of something solid.

My gaze follows the white pillar down to the square and my chest tightens as I realize everyone in the open square below is gone, disappeared, except for a solitary figure.

It's someone wearing black. A boy. And he's walking

toward the pillar of light. Each step makes him harder to see. I watch closely as he draws closer, until the light swallows him completely.

Then, as suddenly as it appeared, the pillar vanishes. It leaves a column of bright light imprinted on my vision.

"That's the end," Sarai says, turning to our class. "Everyone take your seats."

Each of us finds our way back to our desks. I have a million new questions. For starters, how could sixty people vaporize in an instant, and how could this one person be swallowed by a pillar of light?

Sarai stands before us. "Did anyone notice anything different?"

"Blue got separated," Max answers. His face is pale, his voice weak. "And it looked like every single one of us was lost."

"It was not a good showing," Sarai agrees. "I saw two from our tower get captured. And we didn't capture anyone. That puts us down two. Those who didn't make it out will reset, even one from fourth class." She sighs. "We've been losing a lot lately. Could anyone tell who won?"

Kiyo raises her hand. "Yellow surrounded a cluster of Black at the end. I think they may have captured them all."

"No," Helena says, "I think Red knocked out the most. Which one wins if Red got more, but Yellow held the center position?"

"Black won. Again." Sarai crosses her arms, thinking. "They sent someone into the White Tower. This is first time I've seen someone sent up in quite some time…"

"You mean that light we saw?" Kiyo asks. "Where does it

go?"

"To the place that's to come," Sarai says, her gaze distant. "But it can only happen when a tower is above balance. There won't be any chance of that for Blue for a long time. I've told you, no one can leave until you learn to work together. You won't survive long if you become isolated. You have to trust each other." She pauses, making sure she has our attention. "That will be your greatest challenge in the Scouring."

"*Why?*" The question bursts out of my lips, the prelude to the thousand *whys* racing through my mind.

Sarai shakes her head. "Remember, that is the question I cannot answer. I teach you *what* the Scouring is, and *how* to survive it, maybe even to win. Abram shows you *why*."

"Okay, but—" I try to force my questions into *whats* and *hows*. "How did everyone just disappear at the end, except that one person? How was he *sent up*?"

"It's how the Scouring works," Sarai answers, matter-of-fact. "Once the time is up or enough captures have been made, the fight is over. The rules are strict. But the process is forgiving."

Her riddles raise only more questions. "What's the point of all this?"

"To scour your past, of course. Abram will show you when you're ready." She turns to the wall of glass and the four towers beyond. "But none of it matters if you can't survive out there. "

# 11

AFTER CLASS KIYO leads me back to my room. Once we reach the door, I ask her to stay. The thought of being alone, locked in this room with my questions, terrifies me.

She agrees to talk for a while. I sit on my bed, head falling into my hands. "I don't understand what's happening."

She sits beside me, and her hand pats my back. "It's okay. Everything's going to be fine."

I lift my head and turn to her. "How do you know that?"

"I don't know what's coming, but I know what was before. I've seen inside the Sieve." Her voice is soft, distant. "I learned who I was."

"How?"

"It's some kind of magic." She shrugs. "You heard Helena's story. The Sieve shows us who we were before we came here."

"Who we were?" I meet Kiyo's dark and innocent eyes. "So who were you?"

She shakes her head, then sighs. "I haven't told anyone this, and I don't know it all."

"Is Kiyo your real name?"

"Yes. I used to be...Kiyo Shime."

The name makes me smile. "I like that."

She breathes in deeply. "It stays between us. All of this does. Promise not to tell anyone?"

"Yes."

She falls quiet, then her eyes close. "It started in the snow," she says, as if describing a dream. "A line of us, maybe thirty total, were walking in the snow. Sometimes it felt like wading through water, the drifts were so deep. I was near the end, with four children around me, and one wrapped close to me, a baby at my chest. The wind tore at my cloak, my feet were freezing, my legs aching. It was even harder for the children, my children. I couldn't carry them all. The adults took turns carrying as they could, but no one had much strength. Even my second youngest, a girl no more than five years old, had to walk most of the way. It was very slow going. We passed over mountains and through valleys. We were trying to get away from something, some danger. All I remember is that someone was chasing us, wanting to kill us, for what we believed. But I don't even remember what I believed, or why it mattered so much.

"After several horrible, freezing days, we reached a small village deep in the mountains. Fifty peasants lived there. All but five of us had survived the journey. We built huts out of wood and straw. We ate potatoes and any other roots we could find. There was a little rice that had been stored. We handled it like gold. During the days I sent my two oldest sons out to find wood. Their soft hands became hard with calluses. The smiling faces of their childhood wore away. We spent our nights huddled close to the fire. It was so cold.

"I remember one night clearly. The snow had stopped,

though it was still deep at our feet. The moon was full. The mountains around us were white and silver. It felt as if the pain had frozen away, leaving a moment where only the beauty remained. It was that night when a man came to our village. He wore a long black robe and had a different face—blue eyes and a thick brown beard. He was not from our country. Everyone called him San Pedro. Many of the men in our village insisted that he leave. They pointed to a cross hanging from his neck and swore he would bring death and destruction to us. But he had brought many useful things. Food and tools filled his pack. He gave my oldest son—Omaki...his name was Omaki, he was twelve years old, he was so brave, so beautiful—the man gave Omaki a small bow and showed him how to use it.

"Omaki practiced every day. He began to bring home rabbits from the mountains. The man with the black robe began staying in the small hut with our family. I remember the way he slept, on his back with his face up to the sky and a hand clasped over the cross at his neck. He whispered in his sleep words I could not understand. He was kind and gentle. I think he loved me. I think I loved him. But he never touched me, at least, not in the way I wanted. We survived that first winter together.

"It was the next winter when they came. The villagers had been right. The things that San Pedro believed and taught were like poison to our rulers, and they did whatever it took to extract it. They sent soldiers at night. They took San Pedro...and Omaki. I never saw them again. It felt like the snow never stopped, never melted. I stayed cold as ice inside."

Kiyo's eyes open. Her face no longer seems innocent. There is a deep sadness in her.

"You had children," I say, as gently as I can. "How is that possible?"

"This was long ago. Before this place."

"But we are so young."

"I think we all arrive here at the same age," she says. "I told you what I saw. The Sieve did not bring all of my memories back. Only those associated with that time in the village. With San Pedro and Omaki."

"Do you know when this was, or where?"

"In the mountains," she says. "A different place and time. That's all that matters."

"How did you get here?"

"The same way we all did. I appeared in the cavern below, in the water. I swam to the shore and met Abram. He showed me this memory in the Sieve. He told me to tell no one, except you, if you asked."

I put my hand over hers. It feels cold. "Why is this happening to us?"

"Abram told me to consider what I'd seen in the Sieve. I have been considering it, reliving the hurt. I think the coldness in me has to change."

"But how can that happen here?"

"Sarai says it's a process. The Scouring is part of it."

"Fighting against the other towers?"

"I doubt it's that simple. But we have to get to the Scouring first. We'll see..." Kiyo stands to go.

"Please don't leave."

"I'm sorry, I need some time to think." She pauses.

"Thank you for listening. It's the first time I have spoken of this. It helped. I don't feel as cold now." Her expression has thawed, a small smile touching her lips. "I hope you'll get to visit the Sieve. Even painful memories are better than none."

# 12

AFTER KIYO LEAVES, the walls start to feel tight around me. I try again to open the door to my room, like Kiyo did the day before. My hand presses in the same spot. I envision it opening. Frustration builds and channels into wind, but it blasts uselessly against the wood. The door doesn't budge.

I climb into the window and breathe the salty air and watch mist rising from the sea below. It's darker outside. Each moment it seems to get darker still.

The cool air feels good in my lungs. Birds swirl down below, occasionally diving into the water for fish. It must be cold when the birds fly out of the water, the wind blasting them. Maybe the taste of the fish in their mouths overwhelms the feeling of cold. Kiyo's memory made her cold. What about this place could change anything about her past? What will my own memory be? Part of me still thinks it could all be a lie, manipulating us, but after Kiyo's story I'm afraid to look into the Sieve. My body is young, without wrinkle, blemish, or scar, but maybe it was not like that before. I could have been older, in another time and place.

I move to the desk and take the feather pen in hand. This time when it presses on the paper, words come easily.

*Kiyo looks twelve years old. She had five children. One of them was taken from her. She is cold inside.*

*I am cold inside. I look twelve years old. Did I have children? Did I die?*

*I had a mother. Had to.*

*What was her name? What was my name?*

The pen drops. My throat is tight, my eyes moist. I had a mother and I can't remember her name. This realization has slipped in through a crack, like a beam of light through the tower's wall. I'm terrified of what will come next. I place the paper in the desk drawer and return to the window, breathing in the salty air and watching the birds dive for fish as the sky darkens into black. The birds are lucky. They are not prisoners of towers or walls in their minds.

When it's too dark to see, I feel my way along the edge of the room and into bed. Dreams come about the Blue Tower, but nothing before. In one dream Max and I stand facing each other on the top of the tower. I summon the wind to blast him off. He falls into darkness, then reappears exactly where he was. I throw him off the tower again, and he reappears. Over and over and over.

The room is light when I wake. Outside the sky is a dull, steady gray. There has been no sign of the sun, the moon, or the stars. But it's been only two days here. Maybe it's just cloudy by the sea. I'd rather believe that than consider the alternatives.

Someone has brought food again—a loaf of bread and a cup of milk. Bread in hand, I sit in the window and eat.

When Kiyo finally comes, it feels like routine. Neither of us speaks of her story. I tell her about my attempt to open the door and ask her how she did it. She explains that there's a latch inside the stone beside the door. She forms the air into a little whip, as much as she can control, to flick the latch open. She says I should be able to do it, especially since no one has seen anyone harness the air like I did against Max.

I try to open it again. But I can't make it work.

"Maybe that's why they assigned me to get you," she says with a laugh. She goes through the steps again, slowly, and eventually I open it myself. One bar of the prison gate removed.

We walk together up the path to the classroom. Sarai is there, waiting for us. The same group is here, with one difference.

Max is gone. A new boy has taken his place.

Before Kiyo and I take our seats, Sarai announces, "No need to get settled. We're going out of the tower today. You have two days until your first Scouring, and we need to make sure you're ready."

A murmur of excitement spreads around as we follow Sarai out of the classroom. She leads us down the long path through the tower and out a weathered door. We're greeted by a gust of wind from the ocean. The salty spray wastes no time in moistening my robe.

Before us, bobbing up and down in the water, are two wooden boats tied to a pier. The boats have masts rising high from their center, with sails rolled tight at the bottom. Oars stick out from the boats' sides. Six oars per side.

One of the boats has another group of twelve students. Abram stands with them, his gray beard blowing in the wind.

It's another team. And one of them is Max.

# 13

THE OTHER TEAM unties its boat and shoves off the pier. Their oars drop into the water and sweep forward. The boat begins to glide out into the water.

"Let's go," Sarai says. "First a little warmup. Then we'll race."

Our group of twelve steps into the other boat. Its wooden deck is polished and smooth. Sarai directs each of us into an assigned seat. I have the back left, directly behind Helena. Kiyo takes the seat four rows in front of me. Hank is on my row, to my right.

A wooden shaft rises at eye level. I run my hands along it, feeling the smooth grain. I wonder how many kids have sat here. I guess it's thousands or more. The seat feels worn. The grooves worn into the oar's handle seem custom fit for small hands.

Once we're settled in our spots, Sarai unties the boat and stands at the back, with a hand on the tiller to steer. The tower looms behind her. It's all ocean and sky behind us.

"Pull!" she calls out.

I grip the oar firmly and pull. The boat jerks into motion.

"Now lift, in a circle. Like this." Sarai holds her two arms out, showing us how to lever the oar up and out of the water, and back in again.

"Not bad," she says. "Pull!"

I keep my eyes on her and feel the heavy drag of the water on the oar. It feels thick as syrup, and my arms feel weak as toothpicks.

"Pull, harder!"

The boat is gliding now. Sarai steers us straight. We're well behind the other boat, but keeping pace.

"Every time my hand lowers, you pull." Sarai's arm is rising and falling in a slow, steady rhythm. And we're doing our best to follow it. My arms strain, but settle into it. After we've been rowing for a few minutes, I already know I'll be sore tomorrow.

"There are two rules for the Scouring," Sarai says amidst the rowing. "First, work together as a team. Second, capture or be captured."

Her hand falls. We pull.

Her hand rises. We lift the oar down and push.

"We row today to practice unity. There can be no divisions among you at the Scouring, or you will fail."

"What happens if we're captured?" Hank asks. A thin sheath of water glistens on his arms. Unlike me, he actually has muscles.

"It depends on which tower captures you. It depends on what they want to do with you. It depends on your past. But usually, they'll wipe your memories and make you start over." Sarai's hand rises and falls.

"But Blue doesn't wipe everyone clean," I say, remembering Shelley from third class, and her servant Adele with the silver collar around her neck. Bad as that collar is, it seems better than getting wiped.

"We give the ones we capture a chance to convert," Sarai says. "Blue respects the mind. Now, pull!"

*Respect the mind.* I like that.

The oars sweep together. My arms are aching. My hands are starting to feel raw. The tower has grown small in the distance. We have already gone a long way, too far to swim back.

After a few more strokes, Sarai tells us to take a break. "Good warmup," she says. "You should have a feel for it now."

"More than I'd like," Helena mutters in front of me, resting on her oar.

I glance over my shoulder. The other boat has stopped ahead, turned back toward the tower, its oars motionless. Their group watches us float closer. Sarai tosses a rope to Abram, who pulls it to turn our boat to face the same direction as his. They both draw the rope in until the boats bump together.

Max is only a few feet away from me in the other boat. Beads of sweat cover his forehead. He keeps his eyes away. The kids in his boat look bigger and stronger than our group. Most wear the robes of second class, but a few have three stripes on their sleeves.

"Greetings," Abram says, his voice carrying over the ocean, as our boats rock together on the waves. "This race is similar to the Scouring in two important ways: you must work together, and only one team can win." He holds up his staff, the blue orb reflecting the color of the sea, and points it back to the tower. "All you have to do is reach the dock first. May the fastest boat win."

"What do the winners get?" Max asks.

"The Scouring, and this." Abram pulls a small note from the pocket of his robe and holds it up. He looks like he might be smiling under his beard.

*Great, the Scouring and another piece of paper.* I'm struck by a crazy idea that I could just jump off the boat now and sink to the bottom of the sea and it wouldn't make any difference. Why go through with what they want?

"And for the losers..." Abram continues, his blue eyes passing over each of us. "Remember where you began in the tower? The losers return there, with their minds cleared again. You get as many tries as it takes."

I shudder, remembering the dark water in the cavern, the immense wall of stone behind me, and Abram waiting at the shore. It's like a recurring nightmare, being perpetually born wet and cold, without a past. I want to move forward, not backward. I want to keep the little memory and experience that I've gained.

So I have to win this race.

I catch Max's eyes. He's probably thinking what I'm thinking: one of us will lose, and it won't be me.

# 14

ABRAM'S AND SARAI'S arms rise in the air in unison, drawing our eyes. Behind the leaders the ocean stretches forever. I take a quick glance back at the Blue Tower, which looks like the trunk of a dead and limbless tree on the horizon. It's going to be a long race.

"On your marks," they say.

My chafed hands grip the oar firmly.

"Get set." Their arms drop together.

"Go!"

I pull the oar as hard as I can. The water feels like mud as the paddle drags through it, but we spring into motion, staying even with the other boat.

Sarai's arms rise again, signaling for us to lift our oars out of the water. Then she shouts as her arms fall: "Pull!"

And we pull. Then we lift. We pull again.

We begin to find a rhythm. Someone catches the water at the wrong angle, jerking the boat. We try again, find rhythm again.

My hands hurt, blisters starting to form. My arms and back don't have much left. But my blood is pumping and we're racing. Adrenalin masks the pain.

"Pull!"

I pull, then glance over my shoulder. We're falling behind fast. The kids in the other boat are stronger. Their oars cut through the water like knives through butter. They look like they've done this before.

"Pull!"

Sarai's eyes are on me. The wind gusts from behind her, making her black hair flail. The clouds above are stormy. My mood is stormy.

"Pull!"

I can't let Max win this race. Pulling my oar harder isn't going to help. I'm not strong enough, and Hank can't carry our team.

Another gust of wind blasts into my face. Abram will wipe my mind. And Kiyo's, and Hank's.

I know what I have to do.

The oar thumps into my lap. I stand up, staggering as a wave rocks the boat, and walk to the mast. Sarai gives me a questioning look. But no one said sailing was against the rules. I feel the group's eyes on me. They're still rowing.

I reach up to the canvas at the base of the mast, untying the ropes around it. A long line dangles from a pulley above and a sail surges up, flapping in the wind. I grab the line. The sail catches.

The wind blows at a sharp angle, mostly against us. The boat rises and tilts hard, like it has been grabbed by a giant hand.

Sarai is sitting down now.

I turn to the rowers on the left. I catch Helena's eyes. "Stop! Now!"

They stop. I look to the rowers on the right, at Hank. "Row harder. Take turns. It'll keep us straight, moving fast, while I steer. Ready?"

Hank nods.

"Pull!"

They do what I say, and it works. They rotate in and out of six rowing seats, resting when they can. I control the rudder, tacking the best I can. I feel like I remember something about races like this, but the memories taunt me, staying permanently at the edge of my mind, just out of reach.

We're not far from the tower now. We're closing the gap. The other boat is only two lengths away. I catch Abram's eyes, looking back at us. He sees the sail. His face reveals no surprise.

"Pull!" he shouts, directing the rowers in the other boat.

But we're faster now.

As the bow of our boat draws even with the other boat's rowers, Max glares at me, fury in his eyes. They are shouting orders, some of them scrambling to draw their sail up. It rises and catches the wind like ours.

Everyone in their boat rows, and our small lead vanishes. They start to regain the first position, stroke by stroke.

"Nice try, loser!" Max shouts at me across the bow.

Other shouts follow, goading us.

My fists clench, but I do not respond. My mind grabs at the air, as it did before when I blew Max out of his desk. I'm tempted to try to blow him out of the boat, but this time I focus every ounce of concentration on our sail and the wind filling it. I begin to pull in streams of air, like grasping for invisible threads.

The air *turns*. It bends around the sail and funnels into a gale force, blowing from behind now.

Tension strains the mast and the sail as I channel the wind. The effort consumes my attention entirely—I do not see or hear anything beyond the air. I lose all sense of time and place. All I know is the wind. Turning. Blowing.

A hard bump knocks me to my knees, shatters my focus. The threads of air slip from my grip. The sail sags. The boat has stopped.

We're at the dock. The other boat is still coming. We reached the tower first.

We won.

# 15

SARAI AND MY teammates climb out of the boat, tying ropes to the pier. I sit back, exhausted, and stare at the shades of blue around me. The water is dark, almost black, by the boat's hull. A gray-blue fin like a shark's juts out of the water, then under again. The sea in the distance is a thousand different shades, reflecting the shifting clouds above. We must have been on the water half a day, but the light never changed. The same flat gray clouds dominate the sky. Still no sign of the sun.

"That was brilliant," Kiyo says to me, hand on my arm. "Come on, everyone's waiting."

I follow her, stepping out of the boat and joining the others on the pier. The other boat is tied up behind us now. Its team is climbing out.

Abram approaches, a knowing look in his eyes. "Well done." He retrieves a small paper from his robe and hands it to me.

"Losing team, come with me." Abram begins to walk down the pier.

Apparently that's it. No grand speech or celebration. The other kids follow him and the glowing blue orb on his staff. I can't keep my eyes off the orb as it bobs away.

Suddenly, someone shoves me hard from behind. I fight to keep my balance as I turn and see Max coming at me. He pushes me again just as I'm tottering at the edge of the pier.

There's no time to react, nothing to grab.

My body hits the water hard. I try to get my senses, but the water is freezing cold. The robe weighs me down as it soaks up the salty ocean. I manage to surge up for a gasp of air, then I'm under again. I fight to tread water, pulling my robe off.

A bump against my leg. I remember the shark's fin.

I fight for the surface. "Help!"

Another bump. Below me there's a large, dark shape.

I panic and start thrashing, trying to get away. A rope splashes into the water beside me. I grab it hard and it goes taut, pulling me out.

My hands squeeze with the little strength I have left. My feet lift out of the water as the immense shadow passes underneath. I curl my legs into my chest, imagining a shark jumping up for me. But it doesn't. The shape descends and fades.

Hands pull me onto the wooden pier. I lay there on my back, chest thumping, staring at the sky as faces ring my vision.

"Are you okay?"

"That was a shark!"

I can't speak. I'm shivering and breathing fast, shallow breaths. My heart pounds furiously in my chest.

By the time Sarai and Kiyo help me to my feet, the other team is gone. Max is gone. Probably a good thing.

"Help him to his room," Sarai says. "We'll send something warm."

Kiyo slides my arm over her shoulder. I can walk, but I'm glad for the support. She leads me slowly into the tower, trailing after the rest of our group and leaving the two boats bobbing beside the pier.

The large open doors close automatically behind us. It feels clammy and dark inside. At least it's warmer without the sea breeze.

"You'll be okay," Kiyo says as we walk up the curling path of the tower. "Sarai thinks it's just shock. You need rest."

"I'm cold." I realize that Kiyo is getting soaked from holding me up. "And now you're wet. Sorry..."

"You won the race for us. It's the least I can do."

This could be a great moment, a celebration, if not for Max. "Next time remind me to stand farther away from the edge."

"I can't believe Max did that. He'll pay for it."

"How?" I ask through still chattering teeth.

"He'll be wiped, maybe worse. I've never seen Abram look so angry."

"What would be worse?"

She shrugs. "Not sure. Maybe another tower?"

I guess I'm supposed to want this. Revenge or justice or something. But it makes shivers course again through my freezing, soaked body.

Kiyo and I say goodbye at the door to my room. She says she will be back in the morning, that I should get some sleep.

Inside, there is hot soup waiting on my table, and a

crackling fire in the small fireplace. Someone must have brought wood. Maybe the Blue Tower's not so bad. I strip the wet robe and wrap the blanket from the bed around me. Flames dance over the burning wood.

Later, after my body is warm and the soup is finished, I reach into the pocket of my robe for the note Abram gave me. The water has blurred every word, making it illegible. I ball up the paper and toss it into the fire. In a flash of heat it turns to ashes. Still, it's another day without getting wiped. I fall into my bed, feeling a little less alone.

# 16

I WAKE UP under a shadow. Dim blue light fills my room, and a dark silhouette is cast over my bed. Abram stands at my window, gazing out. Long silver hair spills down his back. The light glows from the orb on his staff.

There's a new, clean robe folded at the foot of my bed. It's the same gray-blue as before. I slide it on as I stand, and notice something different. My fingers run along a dark blue water droplet stitched onto the upper arm of the sleeves.

"Welcome to a new day, your third now," Abram says, without turning from the window. "What you've done with the wind is impressive."

"Thank you." Pride fills my voice. "What do these droplets mean?"

"You're the second class leader now."

"Who was the leader before me?" I don't remember seeing anyone with these symbols on their sleeves.

"We haven't had one in quite some time. The Scouring is usually limited to third and fourth class." He turns from the window, facing me. His eyes look like full moons behind his glasses. "I've made an exception for you."

I know I'm not supposed to ask, but I can't help it.

"Why?"

"I think you can handle it, and the time is right. We have everyone that we need in the five towers. The numbers have steadily risen. A few have left through the White Tower, more have come. This has continued, on and on, and now equilibrium is possible."

"What's equilibrium?"

"When the towers are balanced, with equal numbers. This could finally happen, because you're the first to bring our total number to seven hundred twenty. The complete number."

"You make that sound special." The numbers calculate in my mind. 720 kids divided by 5 towers is 144 each. That would be twelve teams of twelve for each tower.

He smiles. "It is."

"Why?" I ask, but already it makes some things fall into place. Like why Abram let me skip first class, and why I'm supposed to lead a group into the Scouring.

"You may not be the last to come, but you are the first number 720. I know this is difficult to understand," he says. "That's why I'm here. Are you ready to look into the Sieve?"

"Yes."

"Very well. Come."

As we take the path up through the tower, my eyes slowly adjust to the darkness. My feet do not adjust to the hard and frigid floor. We pass the door to Sarai's classroom. We pass a dozen other doors, moving like silent ghosts. No one else is out. My ears pop from the height.

The path stops in front of a closed door. It must be the top of the tower. Unlike the other doors, this one has an ornate carving of a water droplet in the center, matching the ones on my sleeves. Abram holds the blue orb of his staff to the door, and it swings open.

A steep flight of stairs leads up to a vast room spanning the whole floor. The walls are made entirely of glass, and the ceiling arcs so high above that I can barely see it by the dim light from Abram's staff.

He moves to a pedestal rising from the floor in the center of the room. It reaches his waist, and my shoulders.

"This is the Sieve," he says.

I step to the pedestal and look down into a small pool of water that fills a bowl-shaped cavity at the top. A small bubble drifts to the surface. Unexpected fear surges in me. This is not just water.

"Look at me," Abram says. His expression is nothing but calm, but it does nothing to calm me. "You will stay under only as long as it takes. I will not let it kill you."

How could it *kill* me? Drowning? I don't know what to say.

"Dip your head in. Better if you go all the way."

"Why?"

"So you can see as much as you should."

I shiver, feeling weak. "I'm really cold."

He motions to the Sieve. "This will warm you up. Trust me."

His hand reaches to the back of my head. The pressure is gentle, nudging my face forward and down, toward the pool in the pedestal. When I'm inches from the surface, I try to yank my head back, but his hand is steady and strong. The water engulfs me.

# 17

I'M INSIDE THE head of a middle-aged man wearing a long white coat, standing in a small cube-shaped room with a woman. He reaches forward and presses a button. It lights up around the number six.

*An elevator*, I remember.

The man's reflection is clear in the metallic elevator door. The name tag on his white coat reads, Dr. Paul Fitzroy. He has wavy brown hair, a long aquiline nose, and dark circles under his eyes. He thinks he is attractive, and I know this, because it's me.

"You stuck here for Christmas?" the woman beside me asks cheerfully, as she pushes the button with the number five. She has a plump round face and radiates with a bright spirit. The name tag on her purple shirt reads, *Patricia Walker.*

"People don't stop getting sick." I hear myself speak, but I can't control the words. I sound dismal.

"So you're a doctor?"

The man turns to her. His eyes—my eyes—pass down and up over her thick body. My face twists into a mocking scowl as I nod in response to her question. "You must be new."

Her face flushes. She stares at the floor. "It's my second week. I'm a nurse in pediatrics. Patricia Walker."

She holds her hand out. I gaze down at it, but don't budge.

*Too many germs*, my grown self thinks.

"I'm Dr. Fitzroy. Chief neurosurgeon."

"Oh." The elevator begins to slow. Patricia's outstretched hand falls to her side. "It's, um, an honor to meet you."

My hands are clasped behind my back as I nod, unsmiling. The elevator doors open.

"Well, Merry Christmas!" Patricia rushes out.

The doors close. I ride up another floor and stride into a medical center. A crowd quickly gathers around me, giving me updates and asking questions.

*Mr. Brown's rate has been dropping fast. Should we increase the dosage?*

*Mr. Johnson is hemorrhaging again. The incision is sound. Should we go back in?*

*We got a new one ten minutes ago. Motorcycle crash. Blunt trauma, fractured skull, but stable. Do you want to come see?*

The medical residents and nurses look to me with fear and respect. I answer their questions methodically, fully aware of my power over life and death with each decision. I still do not smile.

A small group follows me to a room where a person sleeps on a hospital bed. I wash my hands, pull on blue latex gloves.

Leaning over the motionless body, I study a shaved space on the head, around a brutal wound. I take a deep breath as I retrieve two gleaming metal tools from the tray beside the

71

bed. "Respect the mind," I whisper under my breath.

Then I begin to work.

I remember the motions like second-nature, but watching it now is astonishing all the same. The tiny drill enters, the smell of burnt bone fills the room. A scalpel carves through flesh, through brain. Each movement of my fingers is minuscule and perfectly controlled. Everyone's breathing around me is tight.

The work continues for hours. People around me come and go. They provide me with clean tools and other assistance. But it all revolves around me. I alone have this human life in my hand. I don't even know the person's name. But after hours we are clearing out the area, stitching up the incisions.

My body feels immense fatigue as I step out of the room. A crowd is there. A few of them start to clap.

"That was amazing, Dr. Fitzroy," says a pretty nurse.

And another: "No one thought we could save him."

I nod, and for the first time a grin lifts the corners of my lips. The feeling inside this version of me is overwhelming, like a flood breaking free of a dam: *I deserve this praise. No one could save this life but me.*

I shower, change out of my white coat, and return to the elevator. As I wait, I think of the woman who rode up the elevator with me. She wished me a merry Christmas. I can't remember her name, but I know she'll never forget mine.

When I step inside the elevator, everything goes black.

Pinpricks of light spread in my vision, as if I'm soaring away from this infinite darkness. For an instant I glimpse everything—a universe of blackness with small fields of light.

Then my head jerks out of the water. I'm panting hard, white knuckles gripping the edges of the pedestal. Ripples spread in the small pool.

A hand is on my back, steadying me. "It gets easier."

I'm still sucking down air as I turn to the old man, Abram. "What *was* that?"

"It was you," he says.

"The doctor."

"Yes."

"What about the blackness, and the dots of light?"

"Your soul, not long before you died."

"I...*died?*

It seems impossible. I am breathing. Standing. Talking. I look down at my body, young and full of life, less than half the age of the man in the vision. I wipe my dripping-wet face with the sleeve of my robe. My heart is beating. I am most certainly alive, which means I can't have died. And yet...the memory feels so real.

*You died.*

I meet Abram's eyes. "How did he...I...die?"

"You'll learn when you're ready," he says, with the gentlest smile I've ever seen. He holds out a small piece of paper. "Here is your envelope, to replace the one that washed out when you fell into the sea."

I take the paper, but I'm not thinking about it, only about the memory. "Will I ever get out of here?" I ask.

"You have a long way to go," Abram says. "No one leaves without being scoured. Not even you."

# 18

ABRAM LEADS ME away from the Sieve and out of the tower's top room. I expect him to escort me down the path, but he stops in the doorway and tells me class starts in an hour.

"Think about what you saw," he says, "if you can."

I walk away alone. When I reach my room, it's still dark outside. No stars. No light at all.

But in my mind, I feel traces of light poking through the black sludge of my memory. The memory feels so familiar, like putting on an old glove. The man in the elevator—each groove of his movements, his way of speaking—bore the unique marks of me. But older, and somewhere far away from this tower.

*Where am I?*

The Blue Tower. Okay...so where is the Blue Tower? Another planet? Another dimension? Did everyone in this place die on earth and arrive in one of the five towers?

My stomach grumbles. I have that empty, sick feeling of the morning, but still there is no trace of light outside. Abram said class would start soon.

I'm still gazing out into the darkness when the first light

begins to touch the sky. It is like a dimmer switch steadily sliding on, with no trace of the sun, or *any* sun, behind the ever-present clouds.

When it's light enough to read, I unfold the note from Abram.

*In the Scouring, you will bring back Emma from the Yellow Tower. The Blue Tower's numbers must rise, or you will reset.*

I read the note again, fold and pocket it. My rumbling stomach brings me to my feet. I walk and think. *Why? Why? Why?*

I wander back up the tower, working through these questions. My steps take me to the top room with the Sieve. The heavy door is closed. There is no handle. I push on the carved droplet but nothing budges. I concentrate on trying to move something with my mind, like I did with Max, like I did with the wind on the boat. I visualize the door opening, a latch lifting.

Nothing happens.

I step back, glancing down at my young body. It's surreal to see peach-fuzz hair on my arms and legs. I was a grown man. Dr. Fitzroy.

Abram said I have to be scoured. But even if that guy was me, I'm not him anymore. He was a jerk. What he said was bad, what he thought was worse. But…he was brilliant. He operated on the brain. Who was he really? Did he have a family?

These questions make me realize I want more than just to get out of this place. I want to know more about who I was, though part of me still dreads what I'll learn. It seems like Abram is the only one who can access the Sieve. Better try to do what he wants. Capture Emma it is.

I go straight to the classroom. Three of my classmates sit at their desks, talking quietly. A plate of dried fish and bread is at my seat. Someone must have known I wasn't in my room to eat. I nibble at the food as more students trickle into the room. Sarai is nowhere in sight.

After a while Kiyo comes. She sits beside me as usual.

"Nice robe," she says, eyeing the emblems on my sleeves. "What are those?

"Abram told me they're for the leader of second class."

"Glad it's official." She smiles. "When did you see Abram?"

"He came during the night. He took me to the Sieve."

Now others are listening. All twelve have arrived. No one asks what I saw. Kiyo's face takes on the same sad look as when she told me her story.

"The first visit is the tip of the iceberg," Helena says. "I've been to the Sieve three times. Can anyone beat that?"

"I can," Kiyo says softly.

"How many times?" Helena asks.

"Twenty-seven."

A few gasps around the room. Mabel's mouth hangs open. Kiyo is looking down at her plate, crimson on her cheeks. She's definitely not told me everything.

"Good morning, class." Sarai strides into the room, through our cluster of desks. "Today will be your first Scouring."

We watch her, quiet. Our class has never felt so tense.

"Marvelous job with the boat race," she continues. "You're ready now. You'll do great. You may use this time

76

however you want…though you may want to come up with a plan." She retrieves her hourglass, flips it, and places it on the desk beside her. "When the time is done, we go. "

One of the boys in the front row turns to the rest of us. "We have to stay away from Black," he says.

Others start to share more ideas. Everyone has thoughts about how to approach Yellow, and how to keep our distance from the other towers. Half the group, including Kiyo, talks about avoiding Black. Hank is more worried about Red.

"If Red attacks," Helena says, "maybe I'll let one of them take me. That should buy you some time."

"But you'd be wiped," I say.

"We're not all like you, wonder boy." Helena grins, but her eyes are steely. "Some of us have been wiped before. Lots of times. I used to be in Red. I've seen memories there. It wasn't so bad. Red's girls have it good."

*Helena was in Red?* This is a surprise, though it makes sense. She's the fieriest of us. But her idea might not work. Abram's note told me to increase Blue's numbers. If we lose Helena and gain Emma, that's not an increase. Maybe it can be a backup plan.

"Thanks for offering," I say to Helena. "But Sarai is probably right. We need to stick together. So let's plan to stay close to the wall and move toward Yellow. We'll shout for Emma if we have to."

"Sounds good to me," Hank says.

"I'll consider it." Helena leans back and crosses her arms. "But if Red comes, you'll know what to do."

# 19

SARAI LEADS US down through the tower again, single file. This time, after we pass the underwater dining hall and the kitchen, we enter a doorway that had always been closed before.

Inside is a tunnel leading up. It is almost perfectly round, like a dark pipe made of smooth stones. The pitch is steep enough to make me feel like I could lose my footing and slide back down. I step carefully after Sarai, eyes down.

Abram is waiting for us at the end of the tunnel. His head nearly touches the ceiling. "Welcome," he says, looking to Sarai. "Are they ready?"

"Are they ever ready?" Sarai answers.

"The first time's an adventure. Some fare better than others." Abram leans on his staff, taking time to look at all twelve of us. "What's your prediction?"

"I figure they'll capture one or two, maybe lose one." Sarai turns to me, winks, then looks back at Abram. "The group might even get the Blue Tower trending the right way, if they can harness their strengths. What are the chances we catch Green?"

"Soon enough. Equilibrium is coming. It's Black I worry about. We have lost so many to them lately…" He holds his staff to the wall. Its blue light shines on a board hanging beside the door. "This is the score."

The board has neat writing in chalk:

*Black 353*
*Red 128*
*Yellow 90*
*Green 82*
*Blue 67*

The numbers look primitive. Marks of smudged chalk surround them, like they've been erased and rewritten a thousand times. The numbers total 720. Abram said I was number 720. *The complete number.*

But if I'm reading the board correctly, the towers are a long way from equilibrium. When I did the dishes, I counted 67 bowls. So these must be the tower populations. Way out of equilibrium.

"There are 67 of us in the Blue Tower?" I say.

Abram smiles down at me, at all of us, through his long silver beard. "Yes. It's very simple. There are only three ways to leave the Scouring. Usually you capture someone or you get taken. You can do it any way you like. Tie them up. Drag them out. But the captive must be alive. It doesn't count if you put them to sleep."

"How do you put someone to sleep?" I ask.

"More ways than we could count," Sarai muses.

"Sometimes a hard knock to the head," Abram adds. "Sometimes a blade, a fire, a choke. It can be rather gruesome."

Helena's voice comes out shrill. "We could die?"

"Sleep, not die. No one dies here." Abram clasps her shoulder gently. "Nothing to worry about. It's only temporary, like a blackout. You'll wake up back here in the Blue Tower. A clean start!"

Silence falls over us. We've watched what happens in the Scouring from above, but this confirms it. We could be killed—no matter what Abram wants to call it.

"So...if others are trying to hurt us," Hank says, "why don't we have weapons, or armor?"

"Ah, that would not be Blue's way." Abram taps the side of his head. "We have this. The mind. A far more powerful weapon. I suggest you use it."

"You said three ways to leave." Kiyo cranes her neck to look up at Abram. "But isn't there a fourth way? The White Tower?"

"That is not something you can plan for." Abram pauses. "It comes only when a tower is above balance, and for those who are purified."

"Scoured," Sarai adds, her eyes bright.

"If someone leaves through the White Tower," Abram says, "someone new arrives. But only Black has that possibility now. You know what you're supposed to do. We have a long way to go before anyone here will be sent up." Abram turns to me. "You ready?"

"Find Emma and bring her back," I say, trying to sound confident for the rest of our group. "Maybe a few others, too."

"Yes, good. We'll be watching," Abram says, "at least the parts that we can see. Make us proud."

He knocks his staff against the door. A grating sound comes from beside the gate, and it slowly begins to lift open. The light outside is dazzling compared to the tunnel. Abram taps me on the shoulder.

"Lead on, Cipher."

After a deep breath, I step into the Scouring.

# 20

I FEEL EXPOSED, vulnerable as a worm, as soon as I set foot into the Scouring. The ground is bare. The huge blocks of stone at my feet look worn by a million footfalls. Everything is bigger than it seemed when I watched the Scouring from above. The other towers are hundreds of feet away, too far for me to see clearly the faces of the other groups beginning to emerge. The wall around the battleground rises twenty feet above, enveloping us.

When the last of us from Blue walks out, the gate closes.

Everyone is looking at me. I'm the leader. I have no idea what to do. But the others don't, either. This is our first Scouring. The only plan is to stay together and move toward Yellow. It's a start. If only we had something to rally behind. Words come to me from before, from Dr. Fitzroy. *Respect the mind.* Sarai said the same thing during the boat race. It's too much to be coincidence.

"The other towers may be strong," I say to our group. "But we're smarter, right? Let's show them. Let's teach them to respect the mind."

"Respect the mind!" Hank says. A few others echo him.

Kiyo smiles as her dark eyes meet mine. "Respect the

mind."

I begin to lead our group toward Yellow. We form into something like a line along the wall. Movement unfolds from the other towers. The Red tower is opposite us, and half of them have swung to their left, charging along the wall straight to Black. The other half of Red has scattered. Black is to our right. They are marching in military order straight toward the center. Yellow is to our left, and Green after them. Neither of those groups has moved much. If we hug the wall we can avoid conflict, or at least delay it.

Three kids from the Yellow tower move toward us, also along the wall. Our group draws closer and closer to theirs, neither group slowing. We have numbers on our side: twelve to three.

The boy in front of the small Yellow group stops. He has straight sandy hair and blue eyes. He wears light brown pants and a white shirt. A brown satchel is draped over his shoulder. He holds up a hand. "Ho there, Blue!"

I stop. I wasn't expecting a conversation. "Hello... Yellow."

"We are looking for Helena," he says. "We are willing to trade one of ours."

*Trade?*

Abram and Sarai had said nothing about trades, or even about talking with the other towers. I'd thought it was just a fight. I turn to our group, to Helena.

She shakes her head so that her curly bangs sweep back and forth across her forehead. "It must be a trick," she says. "We're supposed to fight. Don't fall for it. Let's attack."

There's shouting and the clanging of metal in the distance.

Groups from Black and Red have clashed near the center of the Scouring. Closer to us, three from Green have surrounded one from Red.

"Let's at least ask what happens with a trade," Kiyo says. "Maybe we can avoid a fight."

Others in our group nod agreement. Hank's face has gone pale.

I turn again to the boy from Yellow. "Why trade?"

He steps closer, the other two close behind him. "Because then we can both win and leave safely."

"You have Emma with you?" I ask.

The flaxen-haired girl beside him registers my words clearly, her blue eyes opening wide, staring at me. It must be her. She's wearing an elegant yellow dress with ripples of silk and lace. She looks kind, nothing like an enemy.

A sudden shout makes me turn. A boy from Red is charging at us, chased by three from Green. The boy has an axe raised above his head.

"Kiyo! Kiyo!" He's screaming her name like a battle chant. "Kiyo! Kiyo!"

She must have reacted, because now he's coming straight at her.

"Come on, protect her!" I shout to our group. A few of us step forward, forming a line around Kiyo.

The boy from Red is not slowing. As soon as he's close enough to see his face, my breath freezes.

It's Max.

# 21

MAX'S DARK EYES are intense, angry. He switches his axe to his other hand and draws a knife. He flings it right at me in one fluid motion.

My feet stay frozen, but my mind races furiously. I focus on the dagger. I gather the air around me and use it to form an invisible wall. The blade hits the wall and falls harmlessly.

Max looks surprised, but he keeps charging at us, the three from Green still on his heels. I have no doubt it's Max, but his expression is blank, like he's never seen me before, like he doesn't remember shoving me off the pier and into the water. Now he's wearing leather armor with fur and a blood red cloak, trying to kill me.

I channel the wind again to blow against him, but he charges right through it. He's too strong. He races past me, swinging his axe straight at the boy beside me, Hank.

Metal thuds against flesh. Both boys tumble to the ground.

Now everyone runs. The Green attackers chase our group, but I have to help Hank. I dive at Max on the ground. My body slams into him, but in a moment he twists out from under me and pins me down. He's staring at me, wild brown eyes and hair spilling out of a helmet.

"Max!" I shout.

He doesn't even register my words. He lifts a gloved fist, coiling back to punch.

I thrust my body up, trying to get free. His fist comes down at my head. I jerk just enough to dodge the worst of it, but still he grazes my ear, making my head ring.

I'm furious as I grab for the air again. I envision a net like a spider web. I fling it at Max and he's knocked off me. I rise to my knees and, in my mind, tie down the net to the ground. He thrashes wildly, but can't go anywhere.

I turn back to Hank. The girl from Yellow, Emma, kneels close to him. Blood covers the ground around them, the axe laying flat on the stone. Emma has her hands at Hank's legs, his robe drawn up and revealing the place above the knee where Max's axe struck.

But there's no wound. Emma stands.

"What? How?" Hank sounds shocked, like someone has dumped a bucket of cold water on his head. He's shivering.

Emma faces me. "We should go."

No one is around us. Kiyo is gone, and Helena, too. Max has escaped, as I lost the focus to keep the net pinning him down. Our group has scattered, except for Hank and me. I see some of them running back for our gate. Another two charge toward the center. Kiyo is one of them, running from two boys dressed in black.

"Can you help?" I ask Emma urgently, pointing to Hank.

She agrees and we pull Hank to his feet, and as he stands he jumps.

He stares at Emma. "The axe hit me...but you...healed

me!"

Emma doesn't say anything. Her arms are wrapped around herself protectively. There's no time to think. The fight rages on in other parts of the Scouring.

"We have to save Kiyo." And the others, if I can find them. I pull Emma and Hank with me as we rush toward the center.

I spot Helena on the far side of the white circle at the center of the Scouring. Many are fighting around the circle, but the path through the middle is clear. I charge straight for Kiyo, still pulling Emma and Hank behind me.

The moment my foot steps onto the white stone, everything shifts. Before, I saw Kiyo across an open square in the Scouring. She's still there, but now I see her on the other side of a hospital hallway. The same hospital that I saw in the Sieve. She's no longer wearing a robe, but the faintly familiar scrubs of a doctor. There are bright florescent lights on a ceiling that did not exist moments before.

"Where *are* we?" Hank asks.

I turn to him, see shock in his eyes and a stethoscope hanging around his neck. Emma looks stunned into silence. She's dressed like a nurse.

"There you are!" the shout comes from ahead. Someone is yanking Kiyo by the arm, pulling her around the corner and out of the hospital hallway.

"Stay here," I tell Emma and Hank, and begin to sprint after Kiyo. I charge down the hallway and turn where she went. Ahead, someone drags her into a room.

I open the door and see five people inside. Kiyo stands behind a woman in a black suit, kneeling by a hospital bed, crying. A young boy is on the bed. He has no hair on his head. His eyes are closed.

Another man stands beside the boy, holding his hand. He looks up to me. It is Dr. Fitzroy. It is me.

I've seen this before. I don't want to see it again. I try to back away, but my body is frozen in place.

*The Scouring is finished.*

The words boom into the hospital room. They fill my mind and I'm sure I would fall to the ground if my body were not frozen.

*The fire will try your work,* the voice says. *If your work survives, you shall receive your reward. If your work is burned, you must be purified.*

And then the fire surges, engulfing me and everything around me.

# 22

WHEN I WAKE up, the ceiling above me is the familiar slate gray stone of the Blue Tower. The room is long and narrow, with short columns. Out of the corner of my eye I see a dozen small beds in a straight line beside mine, like a hospital.

I try to sit up but can't. It feels like lead weights are draped over my body from head to toe. I've never felt fatigue like this, like every ounce of energy has been sapped from me. I focus on my breathing, staying calm, thoughts racing, as my body lays motionless.

I think carefully through everything that happened in the Scouring. Our group had scattered when Max attacked. I'd lost Kiyo and Helena. But I'd helped save Hank. The girl from the Yellow tower, Emma, healed him. Then the moment I stepped on the white circle in the center I had been in the hospital again. It must have been a vision, like the Sieve. Kiyo had been there, with the woman dressed in black, crying at the feet of a sick child. Dr. Fitzroy was by the child's side. This must have happened, but the memory is incomplete. A fire had burned everything away.

But I'm alive again, awake, in the Blue Tower. Not even

wiped. I must have done what Abram wanted, or close enough. Now if only I could get up.

One step at a time.

I focus on my pinky finger. I channel every thought into moving it, my eyes tilting down to watch.

At first, nothing.

A new wave of fear washes over me. Paralysis. Is there anything worse than that? I'd rather be dead, but I already was dead.

One step at a time.

I try again, and my pinky budges a hair. I summon every ounce of willpower to make it move, and my pinkie is curling.

Progress.

Next comes my ring finger, and then the others. I eventually lift my hand ever so slightly, but not enough to rise off the white sheets of the bed.

My next effort is to turn my head. Once I get it moving, gravity helps and I manage to look all the way to my right.

Beside me is Emma, from the Yellow Tower. She is lying still with eyes wide open, staring up at the ceiling. She's wearing a white robe and a silver band is around her neck.

My lips move just enough to whisper. "Emma?"

Her head turns slowly to me. Her lips part, then close. I realize she's testing her movements, as I did. Her lips open again. "Blue?"

"Yes."

"I'm...so...weak."

I feel it, faintly at first, but the more I focus, I sense Emma's weakness, like a dull throb deep in my mind. I also feel her fear, resistance, and awe. It must be the silver link around her neck. Shelley said anyone I captured would become my servant. She said the link makes a servant do whatever I want. In return, it makes me feel whatever my servant feels. This is going to take some getting used to.

Time to test it. I glance down at Emma's hand. "Lift it."

Her hand lifts. Her eyes tighten. "Who are you?"

"Cipher."

"You...captured me."

We are quiet then, staring at each other. She has knowing eyes like Kiyo's, except blue. Her hair is blond, her cheekbones high like a princess. She does not seem to belong here.

I wonder what will happen to her now. If she's my servant, will she agree to convert to Blue? I don't even know why I'm here, or why I'd been instructed to capture her. I don't know how we got back inside the tower. She doesn't seem like a prisoner, because other than the link, she's being treated the same as I am. Maybe we're both prisoners. Neither of us can move anyway.

My thoughts drift again to what I'd seen in the Sieve, and the flash in the Scouring. *Dr. Fitzroy, chief neurosurgeon.* The memory floats to the top of my mind like oil on water. I'd been worshiped. I'd saved lives. Like Emma had saved Hank's life.

"You healed my friend." My lips move more easily now.

She doesn't respond.

"How'd you do it? And why?"

"I'm a healer." Her body remains still. "I asked for the Healer's help."

"The Healer?" I remember the complex movements of

my hands, the scalpel, during surgery on a brain. Healing is not so simple.

"We are only vessels," she says. "The Healer works through us."

My head shakes. This doesn't make sense. I knew about healing. It was my job, my identity…before this place. I healed with my own hands.

Emma smiles, as if sensing my questions. "I saw what you did. Hurling that boy from the Red Tower away, and pinning him down without even touching him."

"Sometimes I can move the air."

"Oh." She is quiet before speaking again. "I've heard that Blue is genius, but also cold."

"I'm not…" I stop. How has she heard this? And is she right, about the genius and the cold? I remember how little I cared about the woman in the elevator. I was cold. Kiyo was cold, but for different reasons. "Why do you say that?"

"It's why my team was assigned to trade me. In Yellow we are warm, loving, healing, but we must learn courage. I had done that. Sometimes too much courage slips into pride. Too much of anything can become pride. So it was decided that I would go. Will my mind become sharper here?"

Her explanation fascinates me. No one has said anything so specific to me about the tower's purposes. "The mind is our weapon," I say. "We learn to work as a team. I think that might be why I was sent here."

She studies me in quiet. "You have also seen into the past?"

"Yes, through the Sieve."

"It shows your memories?"

"Just one so far. Now it's the only thing I know about myself before I arrived here, and it's not good."

"It usually isn't."

"So who were you…before?"

She bites her lip, the muscles of her face allowing more movement now. She slowly sits up, unsteady, her head shaking. "I'd rather not say. There's too much I don't know."

"I understand." It's not like I want to talk about what I saw. Kiyo had felt the same way about her story. She'd left out much of what she'd seen. It's hard to share these things, filled with pain. Maybe I could force Emma to speak through the link. But I won't.

I try sitting up as well. It feels like a giant is pushing against me, but I manage to prop myself up on my arms. Across the room, I see others beginning to stir. No one is standing, and everyone's movements are sluggish. It looks like we've just woken up from a hundred years of sleep. I count them: thirteen total. I can't make out all their faces, as some are turned away, but from their shapes and hair, none look like Kiyo.

"What do we do now?" Emma asks.

"I need to find someone." *Kiyo.* I bend my knees, coaxing my legs back to life, preparing to stand.

"Was that your first Scouring?" she asks.

"Yes…"

"Not many lead their groups the first time, and I've never heard of someone capturing another the first time." The tone of respect in her voice is uncomfortable. I feel her discomfort through the link.

"But I might have lost one." *Kiyo.*

93

No response.

"You've been to the Scouring before?" I ask.

"Yes, I've lost count how many times." She pauses. "It only gets harder."

"Why?"

"Because you start to learn how much of your past still needs to be healed."

Her words have an ominous tone. What else do I have to learn? Already my memory as a neurosurgeon makes my mind feel doused in sickly oil.

I slowly slide my legs over the side of the bed, testing my toes on the floor. It is frigid on my bare feet. Emma is watching me.

"Do you know why we're here, in the five towers?" I ask.

"In Yellow we learn that the Healer must heal our deepest flaws and the wounds inflicted in the other existence."

I decide to tell her: "I was a neurosurgeon before."

"What's that?"

"A doctor. I did surgery on people's brains. To help them."

"Oh." She has slid her legs over the side of her bed, facing me and only a couple feet away. "So we are both healers. It's such a gift, isn't it?"

I remember feeling gifted, like I had the power to save lives. "It's a responsibility."

"No, not ours. The Healer is responsible, working through us."

"I myself saved people. Not this...Healer."

"We can't heal by our own power, because we did not make any of the things we are healing. Only the Healer can do that."

I shake my head, confused. But I just say okay, not in the mood to debate it. I have to find Kiyo.

As I try to stand, I wobble slightly but manage to stay up. I hold out my hand to Emma. She nods and takes it. We stand together and begin to walk slowly, unsteadily, past the other beds.

# 23

EMMA AND I are halfway down the row of beds when someone calls my name. Helena's voice is emphatic but quiet. Her face nearly matches the white sheets of the bed.

"You're still with us," I say, failing to sound excited and wishing she was Kiyo.

Helena's lips open slowly. "Can't...move."

"I couldn't either. Keep trying. It gets better. I think it's what the Scouring does to us. I lost track of you. What happened?"

"A boy...from Green. He took me and...and..." Her lips move more easily, but her cheeks redden as her voice drifts away.

"What?"

"Well, I, um, kissed him," she says. "I didn't know what else to do. I was desperate to get him off his guard. And...he was kind of cute."

"Seriously? In the middle of the Scouring?"

She smiles with her lips pursed. "What? You thought the only way was to *respect the mind?* Some of us can't blow somebody off their feet with the wind, but even I can turn someone's head and plant a kiss. There's more than one way to blow a boy away. And it worked—the boy from Green let go of me, like he was shocked…and a little excited. I had his hand in mine when a loud voice spoke and a fire burned everything. Next thing I know, I'm here."

I shake my head in disbelief. "Maybe as long as no one's holding you at the end, you get out? No matter how?"

"Maybe. And if you have a hold on someone else, they go with you." Helena's smile fades as she turns to Emma. "Who are you?"

"This is Emma, from Yellow," I say. "I guess that means we won?"

"Paralysis is some prize." Helena has managed to lift herself up on her elbows.

"Did you see Kiyo?"

"Two boys from Black had her. She didn't have a chance."

"No…" I stammer. "Are you sure?"

"She'd been in Blue a long time. Maybe she was due to move on. She'll be okay." For once there's sympathy in Helena's voice.

"But in Black?"

"I don't know," Helena says, glancing at Emma. "We use links to control our servants. Who knows what they do?"

Around the room of beds, there are other familiar faces from our group. Kiyo might be the only one we lost, and she's the one I most wanted to protect. I can't bear to think about her in Black. I count the bodies in the room.

"Someone else must have made a capture," I say. "There are thirteen of us in here. Who's new?"

"Me…" a boy groans in the bed beside Helena's. "Jack."

I recognize him as one of the three boys who had been chasing Max when he attacked us. Jack has the same wild look as Shelley's servant Adele, from Green. He has bushy brown hair and thick eyebrows. Even with his white robe and silver band around his neck, he looks…unmanageable.

"You're from Green?" I ask.

The boy manages to turn his head toward me. "Yes."

Helena gasps, "It's *you*!"

He nods, and I quickly understand the knowing look that passes between them. It's the boy Helena kissed.

The two of them keep staring at each other, maybe as Helena gets used to his feelings through the link at his neck. I can sense Emma's feelings turning from curiosity to awkwardness. She's also hungry and a little angry at Helena. I guess Helena could rub a lot of girls the wrong way.

"Emma and I are going to get some food," I say. "Want to come?"

"I don't think I can stand yet," Helena says, her lips curving into a smirk as she stares at Emma. "You go ahead with your new servant, and I'll go with mine."

No one else speaks to us as we leave. When we reach the center of the tower with the path winding down, Emma stops and looks up and down. "Wow…"

"What? Different than yours?"

She nods. "You can't see all the way from top to bottom in Yellow. It's more beautiful there, but this is amazing. So different. It's like they want you to *feel* the height."

"The wind moves through the tower. It keeps the air fresh."

She breathes in through her nose. "Salty."

"It's the ocean. Come on, you're going to love where we eat." I lead the way down, surprised at how the Blue Tower makes me feel proud. It's my tower. Maybe showing it to someone new makes it more like home. There's so much she'll need to learn, and so much she can teach me.

We're a couple floors away from the underwater dining hall when someone calls my name again. The voice makes me freeze.

"What's wrong?" Emma asks.

"It's Abram. Our leader."

"Who is…?" Her voice fades as she turns and sees him. His beard funnels down his chest and to his knees. His eyebrows arc like winter willows over the clear blue pools of his eyes.

"Welcome, Emma," he says, with a slight bow. "I imagine you have questions?"

She nods, and he motions to me. "Cipher will have answers. You will serve him until you convert to Blue."

I can't help but wonder: *what am I supposed to do with a servant?*

"The Healer chose me as Yellow," Emma says. "I will not convert."

"The Healer and the Genius are facets of the same jewel. But very well, you may serve as long as it takes." Abram turns to me. "I will show you your new quarters, fitting for third class."

"Thanks!" *Third class!* That means a better room, a new robe, and fewer chores. Maybe more perks. Maybe Abram will answer more of my questions. "Who is the Genius?" I ask.

"I wondered how long it would take you to ask. He's our true leader, the one I serve. He built our tower, made our rules. He watches us and will come back when all is ready."

"We say the same of the Healer," Emma says.

"Facets of the same jewel." Abram holds out his staff, the blue orb gleaming between us. "In Blue, we do not presume to understand the Genius's purpose, as you do with the Healer. The Genius makes the clouds his chariot and rides on the wings of the wind. He makes winds his messengers. Those of us who hold the most of the Genius spirit, like Cipher here, can use the wind as the creator does."

This explanation, strange as it is, somehow fits. When I've harnessed the wind, it never felt like my own to control completely. Maybe that's why I can use it only at certain times, in certain ways.

Abram slowly swings his staff until it points to me, the blue orb at my chest. "Now that you are third class, you may combine your power with this one's power—" he nods to Emma—"and perhaps you'll survive another Scouring."

"Another one?"

"Soon enough. If you prove yourself ready. Come along now."

He begins walking up the pathway. Emma looks to me, questions in her eyes. It's not like I have answers, no matter what Abram says. But I also know exactly what Emma feels: deep wonder, laced with fear and stubbornness. I feel about the same way.

# 24

ABRAM LEADS EMMA and me to new quarters, higher in the tower. We enter an expansive room with sheer glass walls, like the classroom, except facing the sea. There is a large, wooden desk in the center. An ornate rug with intricate blue patterns covers the floor, and a fire burns in the fireplace. It makes my old room look like a prison. Abram points to a door on the left wall and tells Emma to go there and wait. She obeys without question. Then he leads me through a door on the right wall. It opens to another room with a window from floor to ceiling and a large bed. I run my hand along the sheets. Very soft.

"Like the view?" he asks.

"I do."

"Third class has its benefits, but also its responsibilities."

"Emma?"

"That's one. You must learn to use the link well. You have sensed her feelings already, yes?"

I nod. "It's very strange…"

"Those who come to Blue often do not understand others well. Genius works alone, making us vulnerable to our

101

own corruptions. We need others to keep us grounded, or at least sane. That is why the link is so important, as much for you as for her. Use it wisely."

"I will try."

He motions to the far wall, where a robe hangs. "Your new robe. Try it on, then get some rest. Greater challenges lie ahead. You'll report to a new classroom first thing tomorrow. It's just past the room for second class. Sarai will be there." He turns without another word and is gone.

The robe is like the others I've seen for third class—royal blue with three white stripes at the sleeves. It fits well.

I find Emma in the third room. It's a small alcove with a straw bed and a single wooden chair. No rug. No desk. A tiny, barred window lets in the ocean breeze. It feels like the servant's quarters, which I guess it is.

Emma is standing on the chair, looking out the window. She still wears the white robe that we woke up in. I watch her for a while without speaking. Feelings swirl inside her. They are incredibly strong and gentle at the same time. She feels the same wonder, fear, and stubbornness as before, but now there is a sign of contentment or ease, as if she is accepting this place, and me.

She eventually turns and sees that I've been there, quiet.

"How's the view?" I ask.

"It's nice. It would look better without the bars. I'm not going to jump."

"Sorry, I…" I look down at the cold stone floor, thinking about what Abram said. "I don't really want a servant. I mean, I'm happy to have you, I just…" I meet her eyes and put on my nicest smile. "I don't want to make you do things you don't want to do."

"It's fine. You tell me to do things, and then I do them. That's how it works."

"Are there servants in the Yellow Tower?"

"We are all servants there."

"Under the Healer?"

"Yes."

"Is that a person you've actually met?"

"No. It's like Abram said. The Healer is our Maker."

"So some kind of god, or a spirit?"

"You can't understand unless you've been in our tower. But we all serve the Healer. So I know how to serve." She pauses, studying me. "You aren't acting like a master."

"What should a master do?"

"Order me to do something."

"Ah…" I try to think of something, anything. But I'm staring at her face and all I can think about is that she's nice and that we're in these new quarters alone. It reminds me of what I saw in the Sieve, when the nurse said hello to me in the elevator and I, Dr. Fitzroy, made her feel so small, because I thought I was so important. That can't be me anymore. I can do better. I can make Emma feel welcome.

"How about you act like the master," I say, holding my hands out innocently, "so I know how it's done."

She laughs. "You sure?"

I nod, laughing too.

"Okay, so…you're ordering your servant to be your master?"

"Yes." But I realize this won't fully work. "Unless we're outside these quarters," I say. "Then I'll have to be the master, and you the servant. To keep up appearances."

"Works for me."

"So?" I ask. "What do you want me to do for you?"

"I'm tired. I'd like to rest on your bed. You stay here."

It's not what I expect. Maybe that's a lesson. I can't predict how others are going to act. We do as Emma says, so I end up sleeping on a straw bed like a prisoner again. A third class prisoner.

# 25

MY BODY IS sore the next morning. It's like an aching aftermath of the Scouring, or the straw bed, or both. Emma's door is closed so I pick up a small loaf of warm bread, which someone has left by the door, and sit by the window in the main room with the desk and the ornate rug.

As I eat, it hits me that Kiyo won't be coming today.

The ocean air reminds me to breathe deeper.

*I was a doctor, a neurosurgeon.* The memories still have walls. I saw the vision in the hospital, of the nurse in the elevator, of giving orders and operating on a young boy's brain. The vision from the Scouring was only another fleeting glance of the hospital's hallway, and another operating room with familiar faces. I push my thoughts to the edges of the memories, to what came before and after, to what was outside the hospital—but there is nothing. Memory does not work like a file cabinet, but as an association of images and words. It's like a spotlight has beamed onto the wall of a cave, providing no hint of how big the cave is or of how deep it goes. The echoes of it make me think the cave is immense. As big as a life. My life.

I died before coming to this place. Unless I'm somehow dreaming up this fantastical Blue Tower filled with kids who battle four other towers in the Scouring. Or it could be a virtual reality. I remember from my vision the computers in the hospital, showing charts of heart rates and vital signs, and with that memory comes a flash of what a computer could do. Could it create this reality in my mind?

I take another bite of bread. It doesn't taste like an illusion.

I'm still sitting, with no answers, when Emma opens the door to her room. My room.

"Good morning," she says, stretching her arms over her head and yawning. "That bed is amazing."

She didn't need to tell me that. I feel it through the link. She feels rested, more rested than I am.

"Where'd you get the food?" she asks. "I'm starving."

"Someone brought bread. Probably cold by now." I retrieve the tray from beside the door and hold it out to her.

She takes a piece and digs into it. She looks like a young lioness gnawing on a bone.

"We should see if class has started," I say. "Can you eat while we walk?"

"I guess I'll have to," she says, still chewing. "You're the master once we leave."

I lead her out and up the spiraling path of the tower. It's not far to reach the classroom from the new quarters. Inside, Sarai is lecturing in the front. Emma and I take two empty seats beside each other. I quickly scan the other students in the room. Some are familiar—including Helena—but most are new.

"Welcome," Sarai says to me. "Interesting idea, bringing your servant here, to third class. You're the only one who did."

"No one told me not to," I say, trying to figure out why this would be a problem. Emma gazes down at her hands, folded on the desk. She's silent.

I catch Helena's eyes across the room, and her amused smirk is not encouraging. Why didn't she and the others bring their servants? At least no one objects.

"We are discussing the towers." Sarai motions to the window behind her, where we can see the other four towers reaching up to the gray sky. "Which do you think is the strongest?"

"Blue," an older-looking boy says. "We are the smartest, so we are the strongest."

"Lately our numbers do not support that view." Sarai looks to Emma. "What do you think?"

"Black must be strong," another girl says. "They managed to take Kiyo, and she'd been here a long, long time."

"I think it's Red," Helena says. "Red has passion. They have fire. Their girls can control flames."

"Red is strong," Sarai agrees, her eyes still on Emma. "They have fire in their souls. They have surprised us many times. We are the water that cools, but even fire can dance on water for a time. But I'm asking our newcomer, Emma. What do you think?"

No answer.

"We'll wait as long as it takes." Sarai leans back against a column and crosses her arms. "Cipher, you might want to instruct your servant to speak up."

"Why?" I ask. Sarai is picking on her. It's not fair. "She can answer if she wants to."

Emma looks to me and smiles. I sense gratitude through the link.

"No, she can't," a boy says, turning to us. I've never seen him before. He is big, the biggest person I've seen in the tower, other than the two leaders. He has short black hair and biceps showing even under his loose robe. "No servants may speak before class unless instructed. It stays that way until they convert. Is your servant ready to convert?"

Emma shakes her head.

"So tell her to answer," the boy says, standing.

"Who are you?" I ask.

"I'm Luther, the leader for this class. I make sure we're loyal to each other above all."

Leader, bully, whatever he wants to call himself, I don't like this guy. But it doesn't seem right to blast him with wind and start another fight. And I *am* curious what Emma would say.

I tell her, "Go ahead and answer, if you like."

Slowly, carefully, Emma stands and looks around the room. "No one is the strongest."

Luther cups his hand to his ear. "What was that?"

"No one," Emma says, louder now. "No tower is stronger. All five are weak. They're all flawed. Black is rigid. Red is unpredictable. Green is wild. Blue is cold…and arrogant. Yellow is—" she pauses, as if first noticing how much she'd said. It's very quiet, and all the students are staring at her.

"Go on," Luther says. "Yellow is?"

"We serve. We choose to be weak, we make ourselves nothing."

"Who is the strongest!" Luther demands.

"None of them." Emma's lips press into a tight line.

Luther approaches her, to within arms' reach. "Tell us, girl," he says, softly this time. "Tell us which tower you think has the most power."

Emma shakes her head, defiant. She *feels* defiant.

Luther turns to me, and the look in his eyes tells me to run. He's at least a foot taller. But before I can react, he grabs my robe at the chest, twisting it in his fist. "This is third class. We do not tolerate disobedience from our servants. Tell her to answer me."

"She…already did."

"Last chance." Luther twists my robe harder, and pulls back his other fist. "Which tower?"

I reach for the wind but it's knocked away, like someone slapping a ball out of my hand the moment I pick it up.

Luther laughs. "You're not the strongest anymore, guppy."

He's wrong. I am the strongest. And I'm furious, gritting my teeth and grabbing all the air I can hold. It whips around me and blasts into his face, making his jowls shake.

But still he holds his ground. He pulls back his fist again.

"Enough!" Sarai shouts, storming toward us.

A blast of wind knocks Luther's grip loose. It makes me stagger back and lose control of the air.

Luther moves forward again as Sarai steps between us.

I don't wait. I grab Emma's arm and run. We flee down the stone hallway. When I look back, no one is following us.

But we move fast all the same, winding down through the tower with long, fast strides.

When we reach my quarters, tears are in my eyes. I don't know why. I sit by the window and gaze out at the ocean.

Emma sits beside me, puts her hand on my back. She doesn't need to speak. The link tells me she feels gratitude. She admires courage.

# 26

THE FOLLOWING DAYS dragged like a stubborn mule. Abram visited us soon after the incident with Luther. He told us that we would not go to class again, and that we would work in the kitchen, as penance for unruly behavior. He told me I should be grateful that I was not being reset and sent back to the bottom. That's what he did to Luther. This was not his first outburst. But I would get another chance. So Emma and I worked, day after day, in the kitchen.

"Pruned yet?" My hands are invisible below the hot, bubbly water. The smell of soap barely masks the underlying stench of fish that's been left out too long. If there's a worse smell in the universe than rotten fish, I don't remember it.

"Of course." Emma holds her palms to me. The lines of a thousand wrinkles crease the skin, making her lean hands look fifty years old. She bends her arms. "But my elbows have another dozen dishes before they prune."

"Not bad. My elbows became raisins half an hour ago."

She puts on a good smile for how tired she feels. I ask her, "Want to trade for a while?"

"Sure."

I step back from the sink and take the damp towel from

Emma. She'd been drying and stacking the dishes. Now her hands dip into the suds, scrubbing away at the bowls. Dinner was squid ink pasta with clams, so bits of hardened black noodles cling to the dishes. I use the wind on and off to help with the work, but it takes too much energy to keep it blowing the whole time. Sometimes it takes two or three passes to get the dishes clean. At least the work distracts us from the smell.

I count the bowls as I dry them. Twenty per stack. Four stacks total and we're done. The Blue Tower's numbers are rising.

We leave the kitchen and hardly speak as we make our way to my quarters. Another day full of kitchen work is finished. Abram promised something new tomorrow. That glimmer of hope and the bored exhaustion of three straight days in the kitchen put me to sleep in seconds, even in the small bed. Emma still has the big one.

Hank comes in the morning. He's with his new servant, a short red-headed boy named Seth. I ask how he captured him. Hank explains that he went to the Scouring two days after the first one with us. A troop from the Black tower attacked, and Hank managed to land a punch to Seth's gut, sling him over his shoulder, and run for it.

"Nothing fancy like you and your wind," Hank says, but it's clear he's proud to have made third class. "Blue is up to eighty-one now, highest in a while, people are saying. Looks like you started a little winning streak. Other than that, nothing much has happened while you were exiled to the kitchen."

"So what's next?" I ask.

"Abram's giving everyone in third class another training. He's meeting us at the dock. You ready?"

I'm more than ready.

Outside, the sky is the usual slate gray, the sea dark blue. Fifteen boats line the wooden pier extending from the tower's base. Other kids from the tower mill about. They seem to be grouped by twos. Masters and servants.

"What's going on?" I ask.

"Don't know much," Hank says, "but Abram told us it's another race. Small teams. You two are together, of course."

I glance to Emma. She eyes the water and feels a hint of terror. The wind blows hard, rippling the indigo surface into thousands of white caps as far as we can see.

"You okay?" I ask.

"I've never been on a boat."

"We'll be fine," I say, as if I know what's about to happen. "Come on, let's find ours."

She follows close as we walk the pier. Pairs line up beside the boats. Helena ignores us as we pass. Her servant, Jack, is doing all the work of readying their boat. Shelley works together with her same servant, Adele. It seems odd to be in the same class as Shelley now, since she's been here much longer and learned much more.

The next to last boat is empty. It looks like the others, if a little worn. The hull is maybe twenty feet long. The front half is covered, with a single window in the weathered wood. A mast with two sails rises in the middle. The sails flap uselessly in the wind.

"Listen," a voice booms out over the wind, "this is not a race of speed." Back along the pier, Abram stands at the far end. "It is one of distance," he says. "The towers may be close at the center, but do not underestimate the size of their lands. The ocean, of course, surrounds them all, as the Genius surrounds the mind. But back to the contest at hand. Whoever brings back proof that they've gone the farthest is the winner. You may leave at any time. Bon voyage!"

A few groups move fast, despite what Abram said. They're climbing into their boats and untying. Ropes are pulled, sails drawn tight. The first boat catches the wind and begins to glide over the roiling ocean. It looks like they've sailed before.

I step into our boat, getting a feel for it.

"Cipher, a little help?" Emma stands on the dock, waiting.

"Right." I'd forgotten.

She grabs my hand, squeezing tight and looking uneasy, as she boards the rocking hull. She immediately sits on the bench along the boat's side.

*How do I do this?* I know how this works, mechanically, but the only experience I can actually remember was the last race. And then we'd had oars to help control the boat.

I study the mast, the ropes, the sails. I find the rope connected to the main sail and follow it through a pulley at the bottom of the mast to a knot, which I begin to untie. The rope is coarse in my hands and my slightest pull on it brings tension. So I pull the rope tight, the sail goes tight, and the boat jerks forward. I sit at the back of the boat beside a large wooden handle. It must be the tiller that controls the rudder.

Rope in one hand, tiller in the other, I pull harder. The sail draws tight and I can feel the energy coursing through me.

But we don't move.

I catch Emma's eyes. She laughs.

"What's so funny?" I'd be mad if she weren't so cute about it.

She stands slowly and turns to the pier. Her hands take hold of a rope that is tied to a wooden beam on the pier.

*Oops.* As she unties it, I start to laugh, too.

She finishes undoing the knot and sits back at the side of the boat. We both look ahead, across the ocean. Now we're sailing.

# 27

THE OTHER BOATS are all ahead of us. Abram said it wasn't a speed race, and it's not like I know how to speed up anyway. Unless I want to move the air myself. But it's probably better to save my energy and focus on controlling the boat. I let the wind do its work as I study the mechanics, trying to get a feel for it.

I pull a rope that draws the front sail tighter. It adds a little speed, a little control. The rudder needs only a nudge to shift us left or right. The hard part is knowing where to go.

Ahead is ocean as far as I can see. Rocky cliffs spread further and further apart on either side of us as we sail out of Blue's vast harbor. There's no sign of a dock, a beach, or any safe place to stop. I've avoided looking back, and a glance confirms this was a good idea. We're already far beyond swimming to the tower. Still it stands enormously tall and slender, like a pencil jutting up from the surface of the earth. Except apparently this is not earth.

"Look." Emma climbs out of the sheltered part of the boat with two flat pieces of bread, their faded yellowish color dull in comparison to her hair. "Want one?"

"Sure, how many do we have?"

"Plenty. You should check it out. I'll take the rudder."

I eye her questioningly. "You said you've never been on a boat."

"And you don't remember how to sail," she says, "but you are now. I've been watching you. Looks pretty easy. Sit there, make sure the ropes stay tied, and hold the rudder to keep going straight, right?"

It does seem easy enough for now. I let her take over steering. She guides the boat as I duck through the door. My head almost touches the ceiling inside. It's like a tiny home. Two small cots line the sides and there are a few shelves of food. Bottles of fresh water, flat bread, and dried fish. It looks like we're stocked to last a week.

As I sit on the bed, the significance of all this food hits me. We're supposed to sleep here? How long are we supposed to be gone? A day on the boat might be nice, but a night, much less many nights, starts to feel like a stupid game. My eyes are almost level with the sea through the porthole window. The sky is the same gray-blue as always.

I rise and walk out of the enclosed space. The Blue Tower is even further away, even smaller. The tips of the other towers are just visible beyond it. The five towers aren't that far apart, with each one bordering the Scouring. Yellow is beside Blue, going clockwise, so maybe we can sail to it. It beats going the other way, to Black, or straight out into the ocean that looks like it never stops. I'd rather keep land in sight, even if it's inaccessible cliffs.

When I explain this to Emma, her eyes light up. "I'd love that!"

"It'll be just a visit," I say. "And that's assuming we can

117

even get there. But why not try? The wizard said whoever goes the farthest gets the prize. If we could go and bring back some kind of proof that we made it to the Yellow Tower, maybe that would win."

"Bring back what?"

This could be hard. The link reveals that she suddenly feels homesick. She might not want to leave if we reach Yellow. But she'll have to obey me now if it comes to it. "Does the land around the Yellow Tower border the ocean?"

"I don't know," she says. "Yellow's fields spread out far beyond it, as vast as Blue's ocean. I started in those fields. They stretch for miles, and at the end there's a wall. It'll be a long journey. Even if we find our way there, I don't think we could get past the wall."

"What's between the wall and the ocean?"

She shrugs. "I never went outside the wall."

We decide to give it a try anyway. We sail in quiet for a while. The wind rises, whipping even harder, driving us up and down the huge waves. Emma has to hang her head over the side to empty her stomach. So much for the flat bread.

I keep my hand on the tiller and my eyes on the black cliffs to our right. The Blue Tower is no longer in sight. There isn't a single place where we could stop. Only one of the other boats can still be seen, and it's just a dot on the horizon, much farther out. Something about the open ocean is unnerving, so I stay close to the coast, but not too close. Waves thunder steadily against the rock cliffs. Blasts of white foam spray into the air.

It's much later, as I'm eating my dinner of dried fish, when I first notice the sky growing dark.

# 28

"WE SHOULD TURN back." Emma's face is pale, maybe slightly green, as she lifts her head away from the side of the boat. She hasn't eaten, moved, or spoken in a long time.

I study the waves crashing on the black cliffs to our right. "We won't make it back before night, and there's nowhere to dock between here and there."

"We can't keep going in the dark."

She's right, of course. This dark isn't like the night that I can vaguely remember, filled with soft silvery light from a moon and a sky full of stars. This night will be pitch black nothingness. Not exactly good for sailing.

Another wave thunders against the cliffs. "I could try to maintain this distance from the rocks, using the sound."

She stares at me.

"You know, hearing the waves, we can tell how far away we are...roughly."

She's still glaring. Her sea sickness has her feeling salty. "Can you tell where a rock juts out? What if the wind changes?"

I don't have answers. We're stuck on a small sailboat in a foreign ocean with no place to land and the gaping mouth of complete darkness is about to swallow us. I look around the boat, thinking.

My eyes pass over a rope, and I remember: an anchor.

"Take the rudder," I say, and Emma does.

I scurry forward and pick up the anchor. It has two sharp points, and it's connected to the boat by a long rope. Seems straightforward enough. I toss the anchor overboard, the rope whistling down into the midnight blue water. Down, down, down. This has to work.

The rope catches.

I lift the anchor and it rises like a feather. No way to tell if it hit bottom or not. But probably not, if it pulled the connecting rope out its entire length.

I move back to Emma at the rudder. "We have to steer closer to shore."

She looks past me, to the cliff and the black rocks and the crashing waves. The sound thunders, the wind's blowing harder. We can't get much closer, but we have to try. The sky is still darkening.

I take the rudder and turn hard towards the cliff. The anchor is still down, drifting. *Catch, catch, please catch.* We just need to get to shallower water, but the cliff wall drops so sharply. Maybe there is no shallower water.

The crashing waves are closer now. The thundering is louder. We can feel the ocean spray misting our skin.

"You have to turn back," Emma says, her voice weak. "Please."

I shake my head. "Just a little farther. It's our best chance."

My hand is on the tiller, ready to turn fast. We can't get

much closer without risking a crash. I start to count. Five, four, three—

The boat crests a wave, wind still heavy in the sail, and we glide down. At the bottom we feel it: a jerk.

The anchor rope pulls taut. The cliff wall is about thirty feet away.

I dash around the boat, quickly untying the ropes for the sails. They flap viciously in the wind, and Emma rushes to help. We draw the sails down like curtains. We tie off the loose ropes.

Another big wave lifts the boat and my breath freezes. Just at the wave's crest I feel the jerk again, the rope connecting us to the anchor and the sea floor pulling tight, keeping us away from the rock wall, keeping us as safe as we can be.

I'm suddenly laughing and Emma grabs my hands. We're both laughing, or maybe crying, as the waves crash just beyond us and night falls.

# 29

THE SUN DOESN'T appear—that makes eight straight days since I arrived at the Blue Tower without a glimpse of the familiar red-orange ball—but the gray light of dawn comes and so it's morning all the same. The water is shockingly calm. All night Emma and I rocked up and down, over and over, sleeping across from each other in the little cots inside the hull. Now the deep blue water is still. No crashing waves, hardly a ripple.

It's nice for a moment, a place of peace and quiet. Then I realize the problem. We need the wind to sail. In the motionless air we are stuck.

I'm sitting by the rudder, thinking, when Emma first steps out of the hull. She figures out the problem faster than I did. "What do we do now?"

"Wait for the wind."

"What about your power?"

Of course she's right, but who knows how long I could keep it up, or whether this Genius thing will let me do it. Harnessing the wind is not like riding a bike. *Like riding a bike.* I know I've ridden a bike. It's a vehicle with two wheels and pedals and brakes to squeeze at the handle bars. I remember one thing clearly: little green guards over my handle bars. I try to remember when I rode a bike, how I got it, how I learned to ride it. But the only memory is those little green guards. I loved those things.

"Okay." I force myself to focus. I move into action, pulling the anchor, lifting the sails. "You got the rudder?" I ask Emma.

She nods and sits by it. "Let's go."

The air around us is motionless. This makes it harder to move the air, inertia doing its work, but a few streams begin to flow. Then I reach wider with my mind to gather more of it, visualizing the streams like little currents of water joining into a main, rushing river. The air begins to surge and blow into the main sail. In moments I have it blowing full on, and the boat takes off.

Any time my thoughts begin to drift to something different—a memory, anything—the wind weakens. Emma starts to talk, and as I listen to her words, I lose control of the air, like a slimy fish slipping through my hands.

"Sorry, I need quiet."

I use all of my energy to focus on the air. I try to tie off the thoughts, to keep the wind blowing without having to constantly focus, but I can't. Only my active concentration works, but it works well when it's going. We're faster than yesterday. The water is like glass in front of us, and a V-shaped wedge of rippled waves spreads out behind us.

After maybe an hour of this I feel tired, really tired. I'm sweating and leaning back on the bench along the side of the boat. I let go, take a break.

My eyes close. There's a gentle breeze along my skin but

I'm hardly thinking about it or about anything. I'm bone tired.

"Hey. Cipher. Cipher!"

Someone shakes me awake. I feel like I've slept an entire night. Emma is beside me, one hand on the rudder, her blond hair blowing in the wind. We're gliding up and down big swells of waves. Waves crash in the distance. Billowing clouds stand like gray giants upon the ocean. They seem to be coming towards us. Lightning flashes in the distance.

"How long was I asleep?" I ask.

"A couple hours, but you did well. The breeze was picking up when you dozed off. I figured I'd let you sleep."

"Thanks. It was exhausting."

She nods. "Healing is the same way. The bigger the hurt, the more energy it saps."

I look back at the clouds. "How fast are they coming?"

"Fast," she says. "We don't have long before the storm hits."

"That could be bad, really bad." I imagine lightning hitting the mast, or a wave crashing us into the cliff. I study her face and find calm in her blue eyes. "You're not worried."

"I am...a little." She smiles. "But look."

She points ahead. There, for first time since we've left the Blue Tower, I see a small sandy cove within the cliff—a safe place to land the boat.

"The problem," Emma says, pulling my gaze back to her, "is that I don't think we'll beat the storm. I've been studying our pace, and we'll be just past half way there when the clouds reach us."

As if on cue, a cool gust of wind rushes by. It catches the sail hard, yanking us forward, and then it's gone. I look left and see the clouds closing on us, looking darker.

"Here." Emma's holding out a piece of bread. "You must be starving. Eat this, then you need to make us go as fast you can."

Dread grows in me as I scarf down the food. Then I begin to channel the wind. I feel like a used-up battery, unable to draw as much power as before, but it's easier, too, because the wind is blowing. Now I just have to direct it the way I want it to go.

The sail is tight as it can be, lifting the boat higher in the water and racing forward. We're skimming over the waves, rushing across the breakers.

Thunder rumbles to our left. A flock of white birds soars away from the clouds and over our heads.

The wind is gusting and whipping past us now. The air is getting hard to control, blowing in different directions, faster then slower, then faster still. The waves are hammering the cliff to our right, but we're getting close to the cove. Maybe two more minutes and we'll round the bend of the cliff and the waves can wash us ashore on the soft sand. It looks like a golden nest surrounded by dark ocean, black cliffs, and a slate sky.

"Oh no, no." I feel Emma's terror as she speaks. She shouts, "Turn left!"

I turn and see a monster wave coming at us. It's more than twice as tall as any we've seen. It's taller than our mast.

Emma pushes the rudder hard right, trying to steer into it. "Left!" she shouts again.

I try to grab at the wind with my mind, like trying to control a charging bear with my bare arms. I manage to add to Emma's steering and we're suddenly climbing, up, up, up, the side of the wave.

The boat feels like it would flip backwards if not for the wind I'm blasting into the sail. Then all at once we tilt down and reach a moment of perfect leveled balance on the crest of the wave. In that instant the world explodes in white.

Blazing, burning white.

I'm flat on the deck. My ears are ringing. I can't hear anything.

Emma's face is beside mine. Her expression frantic. Her lips move but I can't hear anything.

I follow her eyes as they move up. Just in time I see something huge falling down at us, the mast, and I roll over to try to cover Emma's body and the huge wooden beam slams into my back.

The whiteness is gone. All is black.

# 30

WAVES LAP GENTLY. A fire crackles.

A light breeze brings smells of brine and smoke.

My eyes blink open slowly. I have a splitting headache, a sore neck. My vision is blurry as I try to stand and focus on the fire. It's a neat pile of burning wood with one exception. A huge beam, thicker than my leg, hangs over the fire, half burnt through, with the other half extending to the shallow water nearby.

On the other side of the fire is a girl curled up tight as a nautilus shell. Emma. Her body rises and falls gently. She's sleeping.

I run my hand through my hair and feel something odd by my temple. My fingers prod gently at the flesh. It feels scarred. I don't remember having a scar there.

I step slowly, quietly, around the fire, to peek at Emma. She is serene and beautiful as she sleeps. She must be royalty, a princess or something. As I kneel down closer I see scrapes along her otherwise flawless cheek, and then I remember.

Lightning. Thunder.

The storm had hit us. The lightning crashed down and must have struck the mast, which fell over on us. It must have knocked me out.

In the shallow water, our boat lies on its side. We must have washed in here. We made it to the cove.

And Emma... she must have made the fire, watched over me, and... my fingers go again to my temple. It's where the mast was falling. She healed me. She had to have done it, otherwise I'd have dried blood or an open wound or worse. Instead there's just a scar that feels years old.

An urge rises up in me. I want to protect her, to pay this back somehow. What to do? We can't stay here, and we can't climb out of the cove. The cliff walls rise far above, too wet and steep to climb. And at the edges of the cove more cliffs extend out into the sea. The water is gentle now, but swimming won't work. It's too far. There haven't been any other coves in sight.

I step into the shallows to study the boat. The hull isn't damaged. Inside, the food is still there but thrown all over the place. I take some dried fish, then return to the beach, sit on the soft white sand, and eat.

I watch Emma sleeping by the fire. The silver band fits tightly around her neck. I wonder if there's any way I could take it off. She saved my life. She should be free. I step quietly and kneel down beside her again. She mumbles something in her sleep, but is still again. My hand hovers over the link. There are no clasps or mechanisms for opening it. But maybe I can use the air. I focus on channeling it as I reach down.

The moment my fingertips touch the link, I feel something different. I feel Emma in a way I never have before. Deeper. I think about my healed temple, about the wind, and about Emma. Abram had told us about the Genius and the Healer—maybe it was a hint about the powers working together. I channel a gentle string of wind and lace it around me and then around Emma, enfolding us. I send an invisible twine gently *into* the link, and then through her mind. My eyes close and I feel it... *her power.*

I draw on it, plucking up the power like a weaver with thread. This thread is fine yellow—golden—as I pull it gently from Emma. The golden string twists around my blue string, coiling together and surging with life and energy.

I take our braided powers and begin to wrap them around the mast in the fire. The mast begins to glow with the same energy as I lift it steadily above the flame, now upright.

My hand wipes sweat from my brow, but I hardly notice. All I can see and feel is the coiled power, pulsing and thriving like life itself as it seeps into the grains and the pores of the wooden mast. It fills the gaps and mends them. Wrapped in our combined power the mast begins to float towards the boat.

Holding the mast steady, perpendicular to the ground, I peel off part of our thread and nudge the boat upright, balancing half on the sand, half in the water.

I'm breathing heavily now, my mind growing faint as I move the mast over the splintered part still rising from the boat. I pull more from Emma, everything I can, trying to cradle her power but not squeeze too hard to make it slide away. And then I funnel everything we have into the separate, broken wooden poles as they come together and heal and unite as one again.

It is done. Emma is gasping, eyes wide open beside me.

I sink dizzily to my knees on the sand, staring at her,

marveling at her power.

"You..." her voice is so quiet, like it's from a different universe.

I hear her saying my name, but it's too deep in my mind to react as I drift out of consciousness.

# 31

THE NEXT TIME I wake up it's full light and I'm feeling much better. I sit up and spot Emma in the water, swimming.

"Hey!" I shout.

"You're awake!" she shouts back. It's too far to see her expression, but her voice carrying over the water sounds excited and...she *feels* shy, embarrassed. "Turn around," she yells. "Eyes to the cliff until I say you can look."

At first I'm confused but I do as she says. Then I understand, with a blush on my own cheeks. She went for a swim without her white robe. I force myself to fix my eyes on the cliff wall. I already feel like I've seen inside her, and even more so after I drew on her power. It feels like a piece of her is still inside me, like a snippet of her golden thread has gotten stuck, woven with mine. The least I can do now is give her some privacy.

Above, there's a bird cawing. The nest is perched on a slim outcrop of rock. A huge white bird descends from beyond the cliff. It glides down easily and settles in the nest. A glistening silvery fish drops from its mouth. There must be a baby bird in the nest. It's funny how life holds on and even multiplies in hard circumstances. Even here. Wherever here is.

"Okay," Emma says, closer now. "You can turn. We should get going."

She's standing by the boat, the dry robe clinging to her wet skin. Her blond hair looks like golden embers when it's wet. The jumble of emotions from her is too complicated to untangle.

"Are you…feeling alright?" I ask.

"You don't have to ask." Her hand moves to the silver link at her neck. "You know I feel fine. Besides, you're the one who's been out of commission for a day. What you did was…impressive."

"Thanks." I don't know what to say about what I did, and she doesn't ask any questions. Maybe it's like an unspoken secret, whatever I did to draw on her power. I imagine the things I could do with our braided powers. I probably could have saved Kiyo in the Scouring. I could capture more people. But for now, I just need to get on the boat. "You think we should go back?"

"No, I feel like we're close," she says. "The storm is gone and it's still light. Let's get to the Yellow Tower."

"How much food is left?"

"Enough for two days, maybe three. We'll sail ahead today, see how far we can make it. If we don't make it to land, then we'll turn back tomorrow, okay?"

I think it over. Not a bad plan. Aggressive, but not bad, as long as there's not another storm. Even our combined powers can't stand up to that. I look up at the mast of the boat. Emma must have fixed the rigging. The sails look to be in perfect order.

"Let's do it."

Minutes later we're sailing away from the hidden cove. We talk some while we sail. There's a good wind, not too strong but strong enough that I don't have to try to harness it, if I could even do that with my fatigue. Apparently I need lots of rest every time I use lots of the power.

Emma is the first one to see the change along the coast. In the distance the cliffs relent. Everything beyond has a golden yellow luster, like it's a land bathed in the sun.

We make steady progress, the wind carrying us easily, until we finally pass the last bluff of the dark cliff wall. When we round the corner, there's a wide plain rising gently up to a beautiful castle far in the distance.

"The Yellow Tower," Emma says.

It's nothing like the Blue Tower. Rather than a single shaft of gray stone, it looks like it's made of bright yellowish stone and elaborate crystal. Its turrets shimmer as if in sunlight, and the central tower has a golden pennant streaming against the blue sky.

"Wait," I say, "Is that a sun?"

"Of course. Did you think it was always cloudy?"

I turn back, studying the sky behind us. It is the same slate gray. Directly above the clouds begin to fade, as if dissipating when they contact an invisible wall between Blue and Yellow. Beyond the golden land and castle, a small orange ball hangs in the sky.

"It's beautiful."

"There's nothing else like it," Emma says. "The stone and glass fit seamlessly together." In her face there's something of her tower—delicate lines like an ornate crystal vase.

As our boat glides toward the gentle shore of dunes, she tells me more about the structure of the tower. How there are pale yellow sandstone pillars inside the central tower and how the glass exterior allows light in. "But it's far from perfect," she says. "Appearances can be deceiving."

We sail straight onto the shore, fill a bag with food, and then disembark. We make sure the boat is secure before beginning our trek up the dunes.

The land is sand and sea shells and reeds along the dunes, but nothing that clearly indicates where we are, nothing that screams: *Take me! I'm from the Yellow Tower.* We press on and come almost to the foot of the wall separating us from Yellow's fields.

I finally spot something that might work. A cluster of wheat is growing out of the soil—the ground now firmer than the dunes behind us. I pluck off a cluster of ripe wheatberries.

"I'm not sure…" Emma is saying.

But a loud thumping sound interrupts her. An arrow pins into the ground a few feet away, its feathered shaft quivering from the force of impact. My gaze follows its angle to the wall, where a single figure stands, loading another shot.

"Hey, hey!" Emma runs toward the wall, shouting and waving her arms. "It's me, Emma, daughter of Chamberlain! From Yellow! Emma!"

*Chamberlain? Daughter?* The wall has nowhere to climb or hide, no gate or door. It's like one long slab of yellowish stone.

I charge after her.

# 32

ANOTHER ARROW FLIES at us. A second archer has appeared beside the first, holding a longbow. Then a third.

Emma is still racing toward them, shouting, but there's no sign that they care who she is or why we're here. They must see my blue robe. They won't trust her, knowing she's with me. They'll probably try to capture us, even if they have to kill us.

I catch her and grab her sleeve. "Stop! We have to go back."

Two arrows pin into the ground just short of us. They're getting closer. We're too exposed. I draw the air around us into a tight, invisible shield of air just above us. I focus on the space above our heads, forming the shield like glass to the ground.

Emma jerks free of my arm. "They might let us in!" She takes a deep breath. "Please, we have to try."

An arrow glances off my shield above, making me wince.

"No," I say, "they'll capture us."

"Then come with me!" Emma's feelings emanate through the link, and they overwhelm me: desperation, desire, friendship.

She wants to go to Yellow, and take me. I'm not ready for this. Blue has become home. "We can't do that," I say. "They might wipe us."

The twang of bowstrings draws my eyes. More archers have come. A volley of five arrows rises in the sky and soars at us. Four of them come up short, but one is a direct hit on the shield.

"I will obey," Emma says, tears in her eyes as she looks to the wall.

Moments later the arrows come again.

As they descend straight at us, I try not to think about what it would be like if the shield failed and the arrows pierced our bodies. I try to think only about the air in front of me, thick and strong as iron.

This time three arrows hit. It feels like a slap to the face, shaking my concentration, but the wall of air holds. The arrows stick halfway out of it, as if floating in mid-space above us. They almost made it through. What if five hit at once?

I turn to Emma. Streaks of tears line the sandy dirt on her cheeks. "We have to run," I say.

Emma nods and takes my hand. "Use my power."

We haven't talked about this. But there's no time to wait. The archers are drawing again.

Holding the shield steady, I begin to draw a thread of her power and weave it into mine, channeling it toward the penetrated spots on the shield. I flick the three arrows out like I'm removing splinters. The shield is whole again. Healed.

Emma glances to me, a look of wonder.

But then five more dark shafts soar straight at us. The

shield is visible in my mind, a blue bubble of air with veins of gold, quivering slightly. Focus, focus, I tell myself, and the shield steadies.

All five arrows hit squarely and pin into the air, the force knocking me to my knees. Hairline cracks splinter in my wall.

I draw more of Emma's power, flicking the arrows away and mending the cracks. The effort is too much. It feels like holding weights above my head until my muscles ache and begin to fail. Emma helps me back to my feet. I can't hold much longer.

Seven bows rise in unison.

The arrows hit, and one of them slices through the wall, but it slows just enough for me to use the air to push it aside, missing my shoulder by inches. I've fallen to my knees again. I reach for Emma's power but can't hold it. Too weak. This time the cracks remain in the shield.

Emma pulls me up and slings my arm over her shoulder. We begin rushing away. I stumble along, leaning heavy on Emma, as I adjust the shield to cover our backs. It's much harder to keep the air together without seeing it. I close my eyes, trusting in Emma to guide my steps, visualizing the shield.

I don't see the next arrows, but I feel two of them. Direct hits. The shield cracks again.

The next hit is too much. In an instant the shield shatters and something hits my calf. Then comes pain, terrible slicing pain deep in my calf. I fall to the ground and the air slips completely out of my control. I grab at it, but fail.

Emma's hands go to my leg, to the wound. I look on in shock at the arrow that has stabbed me. I can't even see the tip of it. But even through the pain I feel the immense concentration of Emma. Her hands are steady around the wound, and the arrow begins to lift out. It feels like someone has lit a fire directly in my muscle, burning and searing the flesh as the arrow suddenly pops out. After the fire comes icy cold. The shock of it makes me jump to my feet, gasping.

Before I can even think, Emma grabs my hand—her other fist clutches the arrow she removed—and begins running. We're sprinting as fast as we can, and when I glance back, I see a volley of arrows crash into the ground where we were moments earlier. We race over the dunes toward the water.

When I risk another glance back, I see another set of arrows pinned into the ground, this time well behind us. We're out of range, and no one's following. We don't slow down. We run as fast as we can all the way back to the boat.

# 33

THERE'S NOTHING LIKE fighting to survive to form a powerful bond. It's the unique crucible of suffering and hardship, making us vulnerable, digging out hollows in ourselves that can be filled with something better, something stronger. I figure that's how it is with Emma. We survived the nights on the sea, the storm, the arrows. She's seen my deep hollows, and I've felt hers. And we've bonded, with our powers and more, whether we like it or talk about it or not.

The sailing goes much smoother on the trip back. There are no storms. No crashes. No broken masts. I ask Emma a few times about what happened at the Yellow Tower. She answers with things like: *I need to think about it*, and *I'm not sure yet*.

Well, neither of us is sure of much, and Emma's feelings of sadness and distance, mixed with attachment to me, mean there's no way I'm going to make her answer my questions— even though I could. Instead I focus on sailing our boat and staying alive. To move faster, I keep a little extra wind blowing from time to time. We don't have enough food left for a slow journey. We celebrate our first sight of the Blue Tower by finishing the last of our dried fish.

When we approach the pier, I count thirteen boats docked there. All but two have returned already. I finger the wheat berries in the pocket of my cloak. Surely we sailed the farthest.

No one waits on the dock as we tie up the boat and climb out. I sway a bit as my feet touch the solid ground. It feels good, firm.

Emma and I walk together towards the doorway into the tower.

Abram appears there, alone. He's quiet as we approach, with a slight smile under his beard.

I pull out the wheat berries and hold them out to him. "These are from the Yellow Tower's land."

"Let's see." He reaches out and plucks one of the berries out of my hand. He peers at it through his black-rimmed glasses. He rolls it between his fingers, smashes it, smells it. "Ahh, wheat," he sighs. "But not necessarily from Yellow. Wild shoots grow here and there on our coast."

"Does this grow on our coast?" Emma holds out the arrow that she removed from my leg.

Abram takes the arrow, studies it. "You reached the wall."

"They shot at us," Emma says, her voice quiet.

"Intruders on other towers' lands are not looked upon kindly," Abram says. "They're usually killed or captured, or both. Good thing they missed."

"Mostly." I decide not to say more, for now, not knowing how to explain that I'd formed a shield of air and that Emma has this miraculous healing power. "Did we go the farthest?"

"We're still waiting for one boat," he says. "But it's been so long. They usually don't come back if it's been this long.

You made it the farthest yet. To Yellow and back. That's a first!"

"So what does that mean for us?"

"A reward." His bright blue eyes look past me as he points.

Following his hand, I see a boat. "That's the reward?"

"It's yours now," he says. "Take it out any time you're free. Sail it anywhere you'd like."

I'm in disbelief. A smile stretches across my face as I turn to Emma and sweep her up into a big hug. She laughs, and even feels a little happy for the first time since we left Yellow's shore.

"You two should get some rest. Here." Abram holds out a note.

My hand stays at my side as I eye the paper. Part of me doesn't want to take it. It's probably more instructions—for the next Scouring. I don't want a next Scouring. I want to sleep for days in my quarters, to have breakfast with Emma in the morning, and maybe to head out on the sea again. I'll take a free future over a known past.

"Remember," Abram says, "you either make progress, or you reset. There's no other way in the five towers."

"Fine." I slide the note into my pocket with the extra wheat berries. The message can wait.

"We'll talk again soon." Abram disappears into the tower.

I take Emma's hand and walk back along the pier. We sit at the end, our feet dangling over the water. The sea stretches for miles. We went so far together.

Her head leans on my shoulder. She has so much power, but also so much weakness.

"You should open it," she whispers after a while.

I pull the note from my pocket and slide my finger under the flap. Inside is Abram's handwriting: *See me at the Sieve, alone, tonight.*

# 34

AFTER READING THE note from Abram, Emma wants to hear all about the Sieve. I tell her the little that I know: it's a pedestal with a small pool of water in it, you dunk your head in, and then you see a vision, like reliving something from your past. I tell her it seems to show mostly things we did wrong, things we should have done better.

"What did you see?" she asks.

I look out over the ocean. I don't want to talk about what I've seen. The waves are gentle, bobbing up and down with a color of blue so dark it's almost purple. "Why does Yellow get sun and we don't?" I ask.

"I don't know. Maybe it's the Genius way—to be brilliant but cloudy and cold. The Healer is more open and warm."

I turn to her. "At the Yellow wall, what did you mean when you shouted that you are the daughter of Chamberlain."

"I…can't say."

"Why not?"

"Yellow Tower rules."

"The same Yellow Tower that wouldn't let you back in? The one that tried to kill us? You're not in Yellow anymore."

She looks hurt—feels hurt, and shy—as she gazes over

the water, quiet. The sound of the water is gentle. A slight breeze brushes over us and makes Emma shiver.

I feel bad for pressing her. It's not her fault. I'm the one who took her away to the Blue Tower, made her my servant. She has never blamed me, but I know she still feels upset about this. And I can't deny: it's partly my fault, for doing what Abram told me to do in the Scouring.

We sit in silence, staring at the water. The wind begins blowing harder, making it colder. I think about how I connected with Emma to heal the mast, and I decide to try connecting again. Our words aren't working, so maybe this power will.

I form the first little tendril of air and try to fuse it with her energy. It feels like dipping my finger into honey.

She turns to me, looking startled. "What are you doing?"

"I'm not sure—wait, what are *you* doing?"

Our eyes are locked as my control over the air suddenly slips away from me—not from lack of concentration, but like someone pulling a rope out of my hands.

Emma has control.

She takes the air—my power over the air—and funnels more of it than I ever could into a giant shape, like a ball. She throws this massive ball of air straight at the water, and the splash is enormous. A huge wave washes all the way up to the pier, but not a drop touches us. Emma has taken the air and, in an instant, formed a perfect sphere around us. I can't control it, but I can see it. The sphere glistens like translucent gold.

She finally releases the power and I fall onto my back on the pier, exhausted, like she's siphoned my energy away.

When my eyes open, she's hovering over me, smiling. "You have so much power!"

"And you...took it..."

She laughs. "Yeah, I guess I did. Not for long though, I could barely control it. The energy was...wow, it was like electricity in my mind. I felt like I could heal anything."

"Anything?" I doubt that. "How about my memories?"

"Sorry, that's different. But I understand now. I could feel the gaps inside you, the hollow places, when we connected. You...don't know who you are."

"That's what the Sieve is showing me, I think."

"We have something like it, in Yellow."

"What did you see?"

She hesitates, but then grins. "Lots more than you have seen. I know who I am, the daughter of Chamberlain. If you help me get to the Sieve, I'll tell you some of it, okay?"

"I can try."

"Good." She stands and holds out her hand to me. "But first let's get something to eat. Using your power made me hungry."

# 35

EMMA AND I stop at the kitchen to get leftovers from
lunch. A huge boy in a first-class robe is there, gutting fish for
the next meal. I immediately recognize his short black hair
and biceps. The name slips out: "Luther?"

He glances at me for an instant before turning back to his
work. There's no anger, or even recognition, in his face. "I'm
going as fast as I can," he mutters.

I stare at him in disbelief. This is the bully who bossed
Emma around, who tried to fight me. He was wiped after
that. Now he's gutting fish and acting like a servant. He
earned his punishment, but it still sends shudders through me.

"Any leftovers we can take?" I ask.

He turns to me with a carving knife held casually at his
side, dripping fish blood. He eyes the stripes on the sleeve of
my robe. "Why are you asking me?" he grunts. "Take
whatever you want."

So Luther's the same. Getting wiped didn't get rid of the
bully. "You will serve it for me," I demand, crossing my arms.

He glares at me, but then obeys.

As he moves to the far wall, where the lunch leftovers
remain, I feel Emma's disgust through the link. At first I think

it's with Luther, but then I realize it's with me, at what I said to him. I sounded no better than Dr. Fitzroy.

"Sorry," I say to her. "But you remember what he did to you back in that class before our trip."

"Yes, but *he* doesn't remember. Be nice."

"I'll try."

When Luther returns with two trays of leftovers, the best I can do is manage a formal thank you. Maybe I should feel sorry for him, but it's nice to leave behind the dirty dishes. They might do Luther some good. They did for me.

We carry trays up the long, winding path through the tower. The other kids stare at us as we pass, like we're crazy or something. News about our boat journey has probably spread. Word moves fast in this place.

My quarters are just as we'd left them. The sky is still gray outside, and I figure Abram's message meant that I'm free to do what I want until I go to the Sieve again. We start in on the food, fish soup, and Emma begins to tell me her story.

"I lived in the 1800s, in England."

I shake my head. "What's England?"

She laughs. "Just listen. It's hard to understand at first, when your memories have such huge blanks. But let me say it all, and I think you'll start to figure it out. It's like staring at something so close that you can't tell what it is, but as you back away, you can see it."

"Okay." I lean back in my chair.

"England was the world's greatest power then, and my father was royalty. Not the king or anything, but a Lord with a nice manor in Yorkshire. We…what?"

"I remembered something…about Yorkshire. Like

Yorkshire pudding, right?"

"We had pudding, sure. But Yorkshire was a region in England, in the north. I bet you remembered the phrase—Yorkshire pudding—because it was part of your language. Anyway, my father was gone a lot when I was growing up on the manor, but it was a beautiful and wonderful place, manicured grounds and all. I had plenty of nursemaids to take care of me."

"What about your mother?"

"She died giving birth to me."

"I'm sorry."

"Thanks. It's weird. You'd think after dying myself I'd get over something like that, but the pain of some wounds seems to never go away. Even with our healing power in Yellow, we have limits." She pauses, biting her lip as if questioning whether to go on. "Here's an example. So I was royalty in a manor. You'd think I could be gracious for having so much. I wasn't. One time when I was young, maybe ten or twelve, I remember being in my room, playing with toys. I had these dolls that I would play with for hours, usually singing and making one of the servants play with me. One night my father looked into my room and said, *Clean up this room, now.* He had this marvelous, deep voice. He started to leave but stopped in the doorway, looking back knowingly. He said, *And I do mean you,* with this obvious emphasis on *you* that made me understand he didn't want me to make anyone else clean up for me, like I usually did. My father always said, *Do not have anyone else clean up a mess that you have made.* Well, after he left I started picking up a few toys, but I got bored. I called for one of the servant boys. His name was Timothy. A frail little boy

148

with huge brown eyes. Kind of like a deer, now that I think about it. Anyway, I ordered Timothy to clean up the toys. He obeyed, of course. Then at dinner that night my father asked me, *Did you clean the room?* And I look straight into his eyes, without an ounce of shame, and lied. *Yes*, I said. I think he knew, and he knew that I knew. And I still didn't care. It was awful. I was awful. You know the phrase spoiled brat?"

"Yes."

"Well, that was me. This was just a silly little example. There are hundreds. It hurts to think about how I acted. Some in Yellow think that's why we're here, to process those wounds, to try to get better. Some think that the Scouring helps us get through them somehow, and then people make it to the White Tower when they're fixed."

I have so many questions about what she's just said, but more than anything, I'm amazed by the feelings from Emma that the link sends to me. She is relieved after telling me all this. She feels lighter, as if a huge burden—mostly shame— has been lifted. And her feelings make me realize what I've been doing wrong. We've gone through all these things—the Scouring, the sailing journey, the escape from the archers— and I have barely tried to understand Emma's past, when it's these things from before that help make her so unique, so brilliant. It is unnerving how much time I could spend with her without really even knowing her. I wonder how much of my life was spent that way, as if behind clouds. I'm afraid to know. I resolve to do better.

Emma is studying me. She looks so young to sound so wise as she told me her past. "How old are you?" I ask.

"You're not supposed to ask a girl that," she says,

grinning. "Take a guess."

"Fifteen?"

"Close. I'm fourteen."

"A while ago you said this was a few hundred years ago. How do you know?"

"They really don't tell you anything in Blue, do they?"

I shake my head. "Guess not."

"Well, no one knows for sure, but in Yellow they try to show us as much as they can about our memories at once. They think it helps us with the healing power. So I saw the full picture of my life in the beginning. Each day is like a drop in the bucket here, and the bucket is those memories. A hundred years here is nothing. We can't feel time pass. I've aged a year, maybe two since the beginning. I haven't been wiped, as far as I know."

"So how do you know how long you've been here?"

"Because of the new people who come. Either from other towers—the ones we capture—or they just show up, like you did in the Blue Tower. These new people have memories from later years in history. In the last Scouring we took a girl from Green. Her memories were from the year 2018, so that's how I know that at least a few hundred years passed on earth since I was alive."

"So it's true…we really are…dead?"

She stands and takes my hand. "Come, let me show you something."

We move to the window and gaze out. The sky is the same gray.

"You remember the sun?" Emma asks.

"Yes."

She squeezes my hand. "I know, it's hard not having it here in Blue. But that's the point. Our memories are from another planet, another time, another dimension. Whatever you want to call it. This place is different. But we're obviously living and breathing, right?"

"As far as I know."

"Different towers think different things. In Yellow, we teach that we fell asleep in that other place and that here we're trying to wake up."

"How do we wake up?"

"No one really knows. But we have to start with our story. That's how healing begins. Maybe if you get to enter the White Tower, that's when you wake up."

It doesn't sound quite right to me, but none of the ideas seem right. We talk a little longer about her story. I learn that Emma ran away from her family and married a commoner, a farmer, and had a baby. She makes it sound like it was a good life, but she tells me only the broad brush strokes, not the details. The details are probably where the pain dwells. Hours later, when it is dark outside, I'm ready to face more of my own details.

# 36

AS I WIND my way up the tower in the dark, I wonder how many times I will go up, and down, and up again. It's the only way to get anywhere in the tower, and it's starting to feel like deja vu. I guess that beats not remembering anything. I reach the door at the top, with the Sieve just inside, and I hesitate, thinking about the cold water and the vision of Dr. Fitzroy lurking inside. I want to know my memories. I do. But part of me would still rather live a new life with a clean slate, here among the towers. Emma might be right about healing starting when I understand my story, but it also means having to revisit old wounds—all the things that seemed so wrong about the way I lived. Still, my hand rises to the ancient wood of the door. Even if it hurts, I have to know if I'm ever going to leave. I knock.

The door opens, with Abram waiting inside. He leads me to the bird-bath pedestal. The water inside looks like ink.

"Ready?" he asks.

"What if I'm not?"

The familiar smile appears underneath the old wizard's beard. "Where else would you go, Cipher?"

"Away from here? The sea?"

"Why?"

"Because I'm free."

"You *were* free," Abram says, pointing to the Sieve, "when you were alive on earth. But your decisions there have left only one path now." A dark shadow crosses his face, wiping away the smile. "Be glad that you made the right choice about what matters most. Your path is up rather than down."

"What's down?"

"We are in the middle place, a temporary place. Down is pain forever. Up is joy forever. But here no one can go up until they've been scoured."

"What was the right choice that I made, about what matters most?"

"That's not for me to say." He taps my forehead lightly. "You have secrets in there. Not even I know what they all are. You have to unlock these things if you want to leave. You have to discover what matters most."

"You expect me to leave?"

"Yes, in time."

Time. I feel it passing, but if I'm reset over and over... "How long?" I ask. "Could I be stuck here forever?"

"Something like that. I would not suggest it."

"So I have to find the secrets inside myself and scour them. What does that really mean?"

"Good question," he says. "I've told you Blue is of the Genius, and this means you dwell deeply within thought, reason, the mind. Long ago the Greeks called it Logos, the Word. It is a facet of the divine, and it abides in us here because of the one good choice we made before, the one that matters. But...those of us who find our way to Logos through the mind suffer a common flaw: pride. And I don't mean trifling arrogance, but the love of your own thoughts and ideas above others. This pride is enmity between you and everyone else. It has been a chief cause of misery since the world began. It has been the source of your desires and it has blinded you from the truth. There is no more dangerous combination than this. That is why you must first be scrubbed clean of your pride."

His answer—the clearest explanation he's ever given me—wraps around me like a bubble, enveloping my mind with the comfort of truth. It fills in the missing pieces of the few memories I have here. Even the recent boat race, to see who could go the farthest, had me wanting nothing more than to beat everyone else. And for what purpose? To show that I am superior? The same thing worked in me, Dr. Fitzroy, in the elevator: the woman beside me had only been a tool that I could use to measure up my own worth. I hadn't seen any value in her by herself.

But Emma and Kiyo have showed me this was wrong. It went better when I focused on them. I can think of no better moments than when Kiyo and I won the first boat race, or when Emma and I combined our powers. How long have they been stuck here? Could I help them get out?

"How is it fair," I ask, "that balance between the towers was not possible until I showed up here?"

"*Fair...*" Abram sighs. "Fair is a misused word. You can only know fairness if you know everything, which none of us do. All I can tell you is that this place, the five towers, were beautifully and harmoniously made for a purpose. And that purpose expected that a time would come when our total number would be 720, twelve teams of twelve within each tower. When you arrived, you were number 720."

"Is that a coincidence?"

"I don't believe in such a thing. Neither should you."

"Do I really have more power than anyone else?"

"Blue has never had a student as strong as you. Others are learning, aspiring to use the air as you do. Our numbers are rising."

"What happens when we reach 144?"

"Perhaps you'll go to another tower?" he says.

The idea startles me. I'd never thought I could leave freely, much less that Abram might expect it. "Wouldn't any other tower wipe me if they caught me?"

He shrugs. "Depends on how powerful you are. Blue's rise will be noticed. Another tower might appreciate your assistance. Wiping you would only set you back."

"So we are more powerful the more memories we gain?"

"In a way. But the memories must be purified," he says. "You are here in Blue to scour one type of tarnish—a very dark one. But even once that dark spot is wiped clean, there will be layers beneath it. That's why the Scouring is a process. It scrubs and rinses, polishes and wipes, washes and dries, until the last of your worldly grime is gone and you leave."

"Okay, purify the memories, grow in power, and get out of here. It's a plan."

Abram smiles. "If only it were so simple. But remembering is indeed the start." He motions to the Sieve. "Whenever you're ready…"

I step forward. My head plunges into the water, and the past.

# 37

THIS TIME, IN the memory, I'm not at the hospital. I'm in a house, a living room, with carpet under my feet, a beige keyboard under my fingers, and a screen in front of me. As my small fingers tap at the keys, words appear on the screen. It is a story, and I am writing it. I type out the final two lines:

*The knight lifted the princess to the back of his white stallion, then the two of them rode together toward the castle. They ruled their kingdom, had many children, and lived together happily ever after.*

I glance at the clock and feel some urgency. I scan the story again, confident it is a good one. Maybe my best yet. There's the dragon, the knight, the princess, but also some excellent twists. The dragon breathes out molten gold instead of fire. This gives the villagers mixed feelings when the dragon attacks. Sure, one person's neighbors are killed and homes destroyed, but a fortune awaits those who survive to collect the gold. Mom's going to love it.

A garage door starts to rise, the sound echoing in my mind in a tumble of emotion. This means a car is pulling in. It means Mom is arriving.

I quickly click the buttons needed to print my masterpiece. I should have another minute while she finishes her cigarette. I wait by the printer, hopping from foot to foot, until the final page slides out and I staple the bundle together. I grab a bright green marker from the kitchen drawer and write at the top: *To Mom*.

I'm staring at my bare feet on the tile floor when the door opens. She swoops in and says "My little Paul!" and wraps her arms around me and sways back and forth. Her smell is roses, mint, and cigarettes. For a moment life is perfect. I don't want anything to change.

She lets go of me. "Sorry I'm late again."

I tell her it's okay, that I understand. Before I can ask her to read my story, she's rushing past me to the living room with the carpet. She leans over the back of the couch, nudging the babysitter. I'd forgotten she was there.

A high school girl with a nose ring rises in a daze. As she gathers her bag, she tells Mom that everything went well. "He was quiet like always." The babysitter tussles my hair as she leaves and tells me she'll see me again tomorrow.

Once she's gone my Mom asks if I'm hungry. I tell her I already ate. The microwave dinners she got are pretty good. She pulls one of out of the freezer. As she's putting it in the microwave, pushing the buttons for 4 minutes and 44 seconds—because that's faster to put in, she tells me—I stand beside her, still holding my story like it's a prized treasure, my diamond-ring gift for her.

"Here," I say. "I think you'll really like this one."

"You're so sweet. I can't wait to read it." She takes it from me and sets in on the counter. "I had a long day, honey. I'm going to lay down a moment. Will you bring the dinner once it's done?"

I tell her of course, but my heart sinks as she leaves the room, leaving my story on the counter. Once the microwave beeps, I take the tray to her bedroom where I can hear the TV. She's on the bed, clothes still on except for her shoes, and a bottle of blue pills is on the bedside table. I say her name once, but I'm not surprised when she doesn't stir. I put the tray down beside the pills and turn off the TV.

I return to the computer in the living room and log into my game. Mom doesn't like me to play, but what else am I going to do? I have friends there who never seem to sleep. We usually meet at night. We go on quests to slay dragons and other beasts together. My avatar is what I would imagine my father to be: tall and strong, blond with blue eyes and a battle axe. I'm one of our guild's leaders, even though I figure I'm half everyone else's age. They know that, but they say I'm brilliant. They say I am the best player they've ever played with, able to handle the most minute and delicate actions with my agile fingers. And in the hours of action I prove it. We beat the new boss—a huge octopus creature that rises from the sea. I lead the charge, clicking buttons five times per second, dodging tentacles, and slicing them off with my axe. The time passes in such a blur that I play almost until dawn.

In the morning my Mom comes to the door of my tiny room. The clock says it's 7:30 am. "I tried to let you sleep," she says. "But I have to go now, honey. Cereal's on the table. Your bus will be here in ten minutes."

I get up and rush after her down the hall, thinking about my story. I'm secretly hoping that she got up early to read it. But it's there on the kitchen counter, untouched.

Mom has her coat on, standing at the door. "What's

wrong?"

"My story," I say. "You didn't read it."

"I'm sorry, honey. I will soon, I promise."

But she's not even taking it with her. "You said that last time…and the time before."

In a few steps she engulfs me in a hug. There's the same smell as last night, except better because there's no cigarette mixed with the rose and mint, yet.

"I've just been so busy," she says, "working two shifts, trying to pay rent and keep food on the table, you know?"

"Do you think Dad will ever come back?" I know I shouldn't ask this. I know the question hurts her, but I wish things were the way they used to be. I wish she could read my story.

"You're my little man now." Her voice is quiet by my ear. "Try to be strong for me today, okay?"

She squeezes again and then lets go and turns for the door. Her hand is on the doorknob when she glances back.

I nod, fighting back my tears and winning. I stand barefoot on the tile floor and vow to myself that I will become a man. I will be like my avatar in the game, tall and strong and unstoppable. Mom's sad eyes are distant as she smiles and leaves me there, alone.

I stand over the pool of water, face and hair soaked and dripping. Water is supposed to clean, but I feel like I've just bathed in gasoline. Taking the towel held out beside me, I wipe dry, but still the fumes are there. I'm shaking my head, going to my knees, crying.

I know without a doubt that what I saw is true. This one

little memory, I'm certain, reflects a lifetime of pain, my pain. And it was only the beginning—Dad leaving us to fend for ourselves, Mom loving me, trying so hard, but failing, and myself having to grow up so young. I think about the story that I wrote, and somehow I know that it was my last.

A steady hand pats my back. I'm in the Blue Tower now. I'm as far away from the memory as I can be, even though it feels so close. I wipe away my tears and take a few deep breaths before standing.

Abram is there, watching me calmly.

"Did you see?" I ask.

"Yes. I'm sorry, Cipher. The world was never meant to be like that."

I consider asking him why this is happening, but I know he won't answer. Or if he does he'll just say something about the Scouring and how I need to be purified. I don't want to talk about it. Reliving my painful past only makes me want to see my Mom. I want her to hug me again, to smell the roses and mint and cigarette.

"I need some time," I say.

He nods. "I understand. Time has no limits here."

# 38

I DON'T KNOW how many days pass after the Sieve. Mostly I stay holed up in my quarters, and when I'm awake I look out over the sea, for countless hours.

While I'm a mess, Emma is a godsend. I told her a little of what I saw when I returned, and she seemed to understand without needing to ask more. The streaks of tears from my red eyes probably told her enough. "I'm here to listen," she said, "if you want to tell me more."

And so she was. She gave me the big bed in the big room. She delivered food and took the half-eaten trays. A few times she just sat with me, in quiet.

The things I think about are both burn and balm. It's amazing how only two memories—a single, painful point in time as a child connecting to another point in time as a neurotic doctor—explain my life. I guess that's how it is with pivotal moments. The events of those early years set a trajectory that we're bound to follow, only the different trajectories diverge more and more as we age. I see now how Dad's absence gave me a lifetime of insecurity. I see how Mom's efforts, while loving, took her presence away from me and made me unable to trust. I see how my gaming was

161

practice for surgery, concentrating for hours on end with delicate movements of the hand. And I see why I believed that it was all in my power, to succeed or to fail, to save a life or not. I still don't know so many details—whether I was married, had children, or how I died. But even with these enormous gaps, I know enough to be grateful I'm here, getting this strange chance to reprocess things, or scour them.

It's morning, maybe the fourth or fifth day since the Sieve, when I decide to tell Emma these thoughts. We are sitting on the floor in front of the wall of glass, as a flock of white birds dives over and over into the water.

She listens quietly as I talk, telling it all, and then she sits quietly for a long time. Eventually she says, with a soft voice, "I'm so sorry, Cipher. It's not your fault."

A bird dives into the water. "I know."

She puts her hand on the back of my neck, leans her head against mine. She says it again, "I'm sorry."

The bird comes out with a silver fish. Water drips as it soars away. My chest heaves in sobs under Emma's tender touch.

"You were a child," she says. "You can't blame yourself for what happened to you. None of it is your fault. The wounds must be healed."

She continues saying these things, softly, comforting me. We sit like that a long time, until my tears stop.

"How can the wounds be healed?" I ask.

"You face the memories, then share them. Telling me this, as you have, allows the healing to begin. It's like letting the sun shine in a place where mold and bacteria have grown. The light sterilizes."

I meet her blue eyes. "Have you done this?"

"In Yellow we get lots of details, little facts and anecdotes. I've told you some of it. But none of it is as significant as what you saw in the Sieve. It sounds like the Sieve helps you cut right to the heart of life—the most important things that shaped you. Without that, I can't make as much sense of what I remember. I can't connect the dots like you've done."

"Maybe the Sieve is a key to the puzzle."

"Like a cipher."

I smile, thinking of the reason why I chose this name for myself. I wanted to figure out what was going on, to decipher it. I'm getting closer to that now, and it wouldn't have happened without Emma, and Kiyo before her.

I rise to my feet and stretch, feeling like one of the birds surfacing after a deep dive into the water.

"Feeling better?" Emma asks.

"Thanks to you. It's my turn to bring you food for a change."

"Yum, fish soup."

"Unless you'd prefer to sail to Yellow again?"

She doesn't. We agree to go together to the underwater dining hall.

I clean myself up, controlling air to dry myself. It feels good to weave the threads of wind together again. We leave my quarters together, taking the winding path down through the tower.

Sarai greets us on the path back down, as if she'd been waiting for me. She presses her weathered ebony fingers against the three stripes on my sleeve. "Glad to see you're well," she says. "Quick as you've risen, you still need at least two Scourings under your belt before you make fourth class."

"Can Emma join me?"

Sarai shakes her head.

"But we're stronger with our powers combined." Maybe together we could even capture Kiyo from Black, if I can find her.

"She is not Blue yet," Sarai says. "But do not worry, you have been chosen for a team that should fit you quite well."

# 39

THE TEAM ASSEMBLES in the tunnel below the Blue Tower, outside the gate to the Scouring. Neither Abram nor Sarai is there yet. The board shows the updated tally for each tower:

*Black 356*

*Red 103*

*Blue 102*

*Green 80*

*Yellow 79*

Still 720 total. The ranking has changed, with Blue in third now. Black has gained a few; the other towers have lost more. Blue has captured most of them. We must be doing well, very well, in the Scouring. The team around me looks confident. Ten of us have three stripes on our sleeves. I recognize most of them, but Helena is not with us for a change. Two have four stripes—for fourth class—and one of them is Hank.

He greets me warmly and then rallies our group around. It's not hard for him to take charge, with his size and his four stripes. He must have gone to the Scouring again, and his servant must have converted, while I was a wreck in my room after the Sieve.

"Listen everyone," he says. "Last time we had a nice haul from Red, and we're gonna do it again. Red pairs up, boy and girl, so we're going to do the same. But here's the thing, some of their girls control fire, so we have to go for them and ignore the boys. A few of us might get taken out. But we've got Cipher this time. We'll stick together, let Cipher tie up a few girls with the wind, and drag 'em back through the gate, real fast. That way *we* make the Scouring end. No other tower will have time to take us, even if they knock us out. Got it?"

It's bold. I agree to the plan. There are a few dissents, but they can't argue much with a fourth-class leader. And Hank said it had worked already.

"Good," he says, as the discussion comes to a close. "Now form up in pairs. Catch one Red and we'll take second place. Respect the mind!"

Hank winks at me, and I smile. It's my battle cry. *Our* battle cry.

The team begins to shuffle around in the tunnel. The other fourth-class teammate, besides Hank, is Shelley. She takes me aside and tells me we'll be together. She also says it took Adele a very long time to convert, but it was worth the wait. In her midnight blue robe she looks like a millstone who would roll over anyone who stood in her way. Yet her eyes are sadder than when I first met her.

"Why was it worth the wait?" I ask.

"I kept seeing the same memory," she whispers, so the others can't hear. "It was about this terrible monster—made of different parts from dead bodies—but I couldn't understand it. I saw it every time in the Sieve. Dozens of times. The monster haunted my dreams. And then, when I made fourth class, Abram showed me something new."

"In the Sieve?" I can tell she wants me to ask. "What was it?"

"I saw thousands of books filling shelves behind me," she says. "The shelves rose so high I couldn't see the top of them. There was a single candle on the desk where I sit. A tall stack of books hid my own face, but my hands were delicate and white, holding the edges of a thick, open book. I wore intricate lace cuffs around my wrists. Somebody outside the room calls out a name, *Mary*. The person called the name over and over, louder and louder. I didn't budge in the memory. I just sat there, ignoring the voice, reading. And then I realized it was my book I was reading. I was a writer."

"Okay…" I say, confused.

"Don't you see? The monster was not real. I created it!"

"The Sieve showed you this?"

"Yes, it shows more the higher your rank. Hank told me to tell you this, and to team up with you," she says. "He said it would make you more eager to capture some people out there and reach fourth class."

"I guess he's not above incentives."

Shelley laughs. "We're going to win, I know it. I can't wait to see your power in action."

*No pressure.*

Nervous excitement continues to build among our team as we wait. People tell little stories, a few jokes, trying to stay loose.

Then Abram comes, with Sarai by his side. As they approach, it hits me that we're missing something. Last time they'd told me to capture Emma. I ask Abram, "Who's our target?"

He stoops down to my level. "No target. That's only for your first Scouring. This time you'll be facing the other towers' best. Hank gave you a plan, yes?"

"He did. So we can capture anyone?"

Abram winks. "Or everyone."

# 40

THE SCOURING IS just as intimidating as before. The vast open space looks impossible to cross. Teams from Red and Black have already started charging by the time our group is out of the gate.

"Stay together. Move fast!" Hank orders.

He runs straight toward the center. The rest of us sprint to keep up.

A cluster of other colors clashes ahead. I search the faces that I can see, hoping to see Kiyo. But the girls from Black wear dark cloth covering them from head to toe. Only their eyes are visible. It's not enough to recognize anyone from this distance.

Hank charges, bellowing, at the backs of six Red fighters engaged with Black and Green. Heads turn to him, surprised. This isn't how Blue usually does things.

A boy from Red swings an axe down at Hank, but I summon the air and knock him back. The axe clatters to the ground. Hank grabs the girl who was beside the boy from Red. Her dress glimmers like fire, only it *is* fire, suddenly blasting from her and toward us. I forge a shield out of air, and I feel other Blue shields beside mine, not as strong, but helping.

We block the fire, but not before it burns Hank. He falls hard, shouting.

I rush to him, now keeping the girl in Red contained in a bubble of air. Others are pushing ahead, keeping the other colors at bay.

"No!" Hank screams. "Take the girls back. Now!"

He wants me to leave him there, writhing in pain. I do as he says.

I funnel every ounce of power to lift the girl from Red. She rises off the ground. She floats toward me, eyes open in shock. I turn and drag her with me as I run. She writhes like a butterfly that can't break out of its cocoon.

People are shouting everywhere. Metal strikes against metal. But the Blue gate is in front of me and I've caught one. Fire burns into the air, as if searing my mind.

The girl has blasted her way out. No, it's a different girl from Red. The one I'd caught is on the ground, her dress glowing like embers in a flame, as the second girl reaches her. I could hold one. I can't hold two.

"Here." It's Shelley, close beside me. She takes my hand. "Use my power."

*But we're not linked?* No time to consider it. I think of her story, delving into her mind, and find a blue thread and pull it from her, just as I did with Emma. It's not nearly as powerful, and not as dynamic in monochrome blue, but it's enough.

The wind gales like the fiercest storm. The girls from Red are smothered and whipped around. Their glowing dresses dim. The fire goes out. I force the gusting wind into the shape of a net and wrap them tight. Their feet drag on the ground as the air pulls them behind me. Shelley's hand is in mine. We run.

The gate to the Blue Tower is open. We race through it, followed by the girls from Red, fighting their invisible chains, but failing. We've caught them.

A blaze of dazzling white flashes behind me. The force of it knocks me to the ground.

# 41

UNLIKE LAST TIME, I can still move. The gate to the
Scouring has closed. The flash of blazing white is seared into
my vision. The two girls from Red stand beside Shelley and
me in the tunnel leading back into the Blue Tower.

As we regain our feet, one of the girls starts to shout, tries
to run, but Abram is there. He holds up his staff, blue orb
glowing, and the girls fall silent. Their eyes fixate on the orb.
Neither of them moves an inch.

"Take them," Abram says.

Sarai steps forward and clasps silver bands around each of
their necks. She turns to Shelley. "Which one would you
like?"

"Her," Shelley replies, pointing to the taller girl, who has
short hair the color of rust.

"Very well. The other will be wiped."

"Wait, no!" I say, eyeing the shorter girl from Red. She
looks terrified. "Let's see what she can tell us about Red, or
the past. Why not let someone else be her master?"

"Only you caught them," Sarai says, "and your prior
servant has not converted yet. So you may not have either
one. Whoever is captured and has no master must be wiped

and reset. This is the rule."

"It is the way," Abram adds. "Lead her down."

Sarai walks off through the tunnel, with the captured girl behind her. I know what will come next. Her red dresses will be gone. She will wake up in a lake in a cavern below, without a single memory. She must start from scratch.

"She will have a chance to rise again," Abram says to me, his hand clasping my shoulder. "You have done well. That was very fast. Maybe a record for the Scouring. And Blue continues to rise."

"It was Hank's plan. It didn't work out so well for him."

Abram smiles. "He's fine. He was still awake when you entered the gate with the captives and brought today's Scouring to an end."

"Where is he?"

"In the recovery room. You may go if you like."

I go straight there. It takes a few minutes, my steps racing through the tunnel and up the path through the tower. A few people shout a cheer and pat me on the back as I pass. Maybe they were watching the Scouring from above.

When I enter the recovery room, it looks exactly as it did before. There are two rows of white beds. Ten bodies move sluggishly under sheets. That means everyone is here, because the other two were Shelley and me. Plus our two captives.

Walking the line of beds, I find Hank and kneel by his side. It's some magic, how the white light in the Scouring makes everyone disappear and instantly reappear back in the tower. A word associated with my memory as a child, playing a computer game, comes to me: teleportation.

Hank's face lights up. "Cipher!"

"You remember me."

"Of course," he says, rising to his elbows. He wears the same midnight blue robe with the four stripes on the sleeves. "I told you it would work. You're strong enough to catch people and get them out fast. All I had to do was stay alive. Respect the mind, right?"

"You were burned pretty bad."

Hank sits up, eyeing his body. "Oh brother, that hurt like the devil... But hey, now I'm good as new."

The way he speaks sounds familiar somehow. "Hank, I know you probably don't want to talk about it now, but would you be up for telling me who you were sometime?"

"Sure, my friend," he says. "Help me up?"

I hold out my hand. He grabs it and pulls, almost hard enough to yank me down on the bed. As he stands, he looms over me by a full head. "I gotta eat," he says. "Walk with me, and we'll talk."

We stop by a few others from our team before leaving. Everyone's movements are coming back. They're glad to hear about the captures in the Scouring. More of them look at me like I'm some kind of hero.

Hank and I leave the recovery room together. As we walk down the path, Hank tells me he lived in the United States of America.

"So did I."

"I knew I liked you!" he says. "When were you there?"

"I'm...not sure yet."

"Well I was alive in the early 1800s. I was a preacher, traveling around with nothing but my horse, my boots, and a thick old book. It was a hard life, cold winters and never

174

having a permanent home. But itinerants have their advantages. I was about as free as a man could be. Maybe too free sometimes…"

We reach the clear glass dining hall and take a table near the center. A legion of jellyfish drifts below us, bumping into the glass at our feet. They glow pink and purple, almost fluorescent. A first-class boy brings us a feast of fish soup and seaweed.

Hank's bowl is empty when he asks me, "So who were you?"

I explain it as best as I can, how I was a doctor long after Hank was alive. I operated on brains. They called me a neurosurgeon, which sounds very impressive to Hank. I leave out the part from my childhood, and the parts where I was an arrogant prick. It's too easy to leave out the bad parts of my story. And telling only the good parts makes me sound like a decent person. Which I was not.

"There's more," I say. "I had a lot of issues. Sounds like most of us did."

"Ain't that the truth!" Hank smiles. "We just gotta figure out what they were, and then scour 'em. Then the White Tower awaits!"

# 42

TWO DAYS PASS without another Scouring or any sight of Abram or Sarai. I tell Emma about the new captures. I have duties assigned in the morning, usually supervising first and second-class students, as Shelley did when Kiyo and I washed dishes. I wonder how I can get Kiyo back. It seems the only way is the Scouring.

The second afternoon Emma and I take my new boat out. The freedom of the open ocean provides a welcome change, but we do not sail so far we can't make it back before dark. When we return to my quarters, a note is waiting. This time it's from Sarai, not Abram. It reads: *Tomorrow will be your first Hunting. Emma may prove herself loyal. A messenger will come and show you the way.*

The Hunting. It sounds ominous.

In the morning a boy comes as promised. He wears a white robe and a silver band around his neck. Emma and I follow him up the path, trying to keep up with his long strides. "This is the Hunting class," he says, as he stops and opens a door.

The room is as grand as Sarai's classroom, but the shape is different. The floor curves down like a bowl, and there's no window. Sarai stands at the front, her onyx hair and eyes contrasting with the light marble floor.

As Emma and I find two chairs, Sarai approaches us: "Servants don't sit here for this class." She points at Emma, then to the back of the room. "You may stand up there, and otherwise do as your master commands."

*Why?* Emma knows almost as much about this place as I do. She's proven herself loyal. I start to protest, but Emma stops me with a gentle hand on my shoulder. She walks away without a word.

I sit in silence, trying to study the room and figure out what else has changed. There's a chalkboard behind Sarai in the front. It has one word written on it: *Hunting.*

There are new faces in this room, and they continue to enter until there are thirty-six kids and not a single empty chair. I recognize several students. Hank. Shelley. Helena. Everyone has three or four stripes on their sleeves.

The servants line up on the wall at the back of the room, standing like sentinels. I count thirty-six of them as well. That makes seventy-two people in the room, not counting Sarai.

She taps a long wooden rod against the desk, calling the class to order. "Welcome to those of you who have just been elevated to third class. Welcome to our fourth-class leaders. Sadly, a few of you are growing…stale. No one may stay fourth class forever without progress. We must make room for others. So the time has come for the next Hunting. If this is your third attempt, remember that failure requires a reset."

Murmurs spread around the room. Apparently I'm not the only one who's never heard this before.

"Now, here is what you need to know." Sarai sits on the

edge of the desk with her arms folded, and continues. "You will divide into teams of twelve, and you will hunt down and bring back someone from another tower. You will do this from *outside* the Scouring walls. Most who succeed find someone who has wandered away from their tower and is near the coast. The sea is our friend. You will take your servants with you on your boats. The first team to return with a captive wins. The other two teams lose. Each of you has three attempts to win a Hunting, and those who do not succeed are wiped clean to start fresh again. Remember, we are of the Genius. With minds like yours, you don't need hand-holding."

She stands and motions to a bowl made of stone that sits on the desk. "Come, it is time to divide. Take a card. Then you can discuss among your teams. "

The students begin to rise. I follow them to the bowl and wait in line. Part of me is surprised by Sarai's instructions. I'd thought the Scouring was the only way to capture from the other towers. It seemed like that was the whole point of the board beside the gateway into the Scouring, to keep a tally of each tower's numbers. But I've been here long enough now that not much surprises me.

The bowl on the table in the front is just wide enough at the top to fit a single hand reaching down. Each student who reaches in takes out a slip of paper. Groups begin to form.

"Ones over here!"

"Twos!"

"Who else is three?"

Simple enough. One, two, three. No reason to be nervous, but as it's my turn to the step up to the bowl, I start to wonder if this is really random. I doubt it.

My hand hovers over the hole at the top of the bowl. It looks like a mouth as I glimpse inside.

"Take your number," Sarai says.

I reach in slowly, expecting to grab a piece of paper, but my arm goes deeper and touches nothing. Just as my elbow crosses into the mouth, I feel water. Then pain.

Something grabs my hand and yanks my arm further down. My feet rise off the ground as I'm jerked by the arm, until it feels like only my shoulder keeps me from getting swallowed whole.

A flash of electric current burns into me, like fire burning on my hand under the water. My body thrashes to get free, but my arm is clutched hard by whatever is inside the bowl.

It suddenly releases.

My arm slides out and my knees are weak.

Sarai holds my arm, giving support. She glances at my right hand, where there's a scar—like an old wound. It is two lines, a long vertical one crossed by a shorter horizontal one. Sarai looks up, the surprise plain on her eyes. "It's been so long…" she mutters, then stops herself. She turns to the students around us. Everyone is staring at me.

"What number?" Sarai asks.

I uncurl my scarred fist. A piece of paper is in my hand. I don't remember grabbing it. "Two."

Sarai points to a group of students in the corner. "They're over there." She looks to the next kid in line as if nothing happened. "Next."

The boy behind me steps forward. I finger the scar on my fist and eye the group of twos.

# 43

HANK GREETS ME with a smile as I join the group of twos. He puts his hand on my back and turns to introduce me to the others. "This is Cipher. He's the one I was telling you about."

They look at me like they're expecting something.

"Hey." My fist is still burning from whatever seared my skin in the bowl.

"Why'd you reach so deep into the bowl?" a girl asks, laughing a little. "It was pretty funny. You made it look like something grabbed you."

At the table with the bowl, there's still a line of students. A boy steps up, reaches in, takes a paper, and shuffles over to the group of threes. I'm holding my burnt hand with my other hand, hiding the scar. The others think I was joking. "I...don't know."

"Well, we're glad to have you," Hank says, turning to the others. "Cipher here is the one who helped us win the first boat race as newbies. And he captured a girl from the Yellow in his first Scouring. And *two* girls from Red in his second Scouring."

"Really?" another boy asks. "A capture the first time?"

I nod, turning to Emma and motioning for her to come, but someone grabs my arm—the one without the scar.

It's Helena. "No servants," she says. "We should know better than to mix with them while we come up with our strategy."

"That's ridiculous." I watch Emma as she approaches. "If we're supposed to capture someone from another tower, then we need them to show us how to do it. Emma and I made it all the way to the wall of the Yellow tower."

"Already?" a boy asks. "When?"

"During the second boat race. The one where we see who can go the farthest."

"You went to another tower during the second race?" Helena asks, failing to hide her surprise. "That's impossible. Those little boats can't survive the open sea."

Emma joins me by my side. "We made it."

No one responds, but they continue to look at me like I'm an alien. Maybe I am.

Emma runs a finger over the scar on my hand, frowning. She leans close to me and whispers, "I can't heal it."

This is not good. I'm baffled at what could have made the scar, and why.

"What did she say to you?" Helena asks.

I shrug off the question. "Nothing."

"Oh? You act like you're more loyal to her—from the *Yellow* tower—than to us." Helena's hands curl into fists at her hips. "They are *servants*, not friends."

I still cannot understand why everyone makes this distinction. Emma is a person, not a servant. People just like bossing others around too much. But I do want the loyalty of this group. Apparently it's important. I try to find a middle way: "We are going to need our servants' help if we're going to win."

"Right…" Helena turns to the line of servants by the wall. "Jack, come."

A tall boy with bronzed skin and dark hair starts walking toward us. He's the wild-looking one who was in the recovery room beside Helena after the first Scouring.

"I captured him from Green," Helena tells the group. "Jack is excellent with the bow and the spear, but he still has a lot to learn about boats."

Jack comes to Helena's side. He's a lot bigger than I am. "Yes, master?" he asks.

"We'll be meeting in the room next door soon," Helena says. "Go catch some fish, cook them, and bring them to us."

"Yes, master." He trots away.

"See," Helena says, her innocent tone plainly taunting me. "I agree that our servants can help. But until they have converted to our side"—her voice lowers as she eyes Emma—"we *cannot* trust them with strategy."

"She's right," another boy says. He has just joined our group, and he looks like the oldest of us with the shadow of a beard. He wears four stripes on his sleeve. He's as big as Jack, and as Hank, and one of the few fourth-class members. "The twelve of us must work closely together. We must trust each other if we are going to succeed. If we don't, we will fail."

"How do you know?" I ask.

"Because I've failed two times before," he says. "And I'm not going to fail again. All of you, let's go to our strategy room. We have to plan."

# 44

THE STRATEGY ROOM looks like a war room. There's a huge table in the center, with two candles beside a large map of intricate lines and colors. It's an amazing map. Some cartographer must have traveled all over and studied each tower's lands. I follow the line of the jagged coast south of the Blue Tower to where it becomes a long yellow beach. It fits what I remember from my voyage with Emma. But past the beach comes unfamiliar territory to the west. A dense green forest stretches to a wide river, and then there are reddish peaks on the opposite side of the circle from our tower. The peaks rise to an immense ridge, which drops to the terraced hills of the Black Tower and then back around to the ocean, to us. So we are on an island. An unnatural, oddly-shaped island, with each tower having its own clear expanse of territory. The divisions between the territories are too sudden to be accidental. It looks like the whole place was designed with the purpose of dividing the five towers. Nothing is drawn beyond the ocean that surrounds us.

"All of you, gather close," the fourth-class boy says. He led us here and introduced himself as Pierre. Most in the group seem to have accepted that he's in command. "We must do two things to succeed. First, like I said, we have to know each other, trust each other, and work together."

"Isn't that three things?" Helena asks.

Pierre laughs, his cheeks a little red. It's not the first time I've seen Helena have that effect on a boy. "Yeah, but they're all kind of the same. The second thing is to agree on our plan, but let's start with getting to know each other. Who was everyone…before?"

Quiet falls over the group. This is awkward. No one talks openly about what we've seen in the Sieve, at least not so soon. Most of the memories are too personal, but maybe it's a good idea. I understand Emma better now that I know something of her past. It will probably help us if we learn a little about each other.

Helena, never shy, is the first to speak up. "I was Helena Augusta Imperatrix. As soon as I learned, I started going by Helena here, too."

"Why not Imperatrix?" I ask, smiling.

"That was my title." Her finger twirls one of her curls in the way someone does when acting nonchalant but enjoying the attention. "I lived in the third century AD, in the Roman Empire. And my son was Constantine, the Emperor."

"That's amazing," Pierre says. "I know all about him. I lived in the fifteenth century in France, long after the Roman Empire, but Constantine was a legend."

"No surprise there," Helena says. "I raised him well. The Empire became very strong under his reign."

I can't help but stare at Helena in amazement. She must have learned this recently from the Sieve, because she never mentioned her son when she told her story during my first lunch with our class. She had only told us about meeting an emperor in some tavern. Now it's not hard to see where that led. Maybe she has the same mix of pride and pain that I have in my past. We probably all do.

"So who's next?" Pierre asks, his gaze shifting to the boy standing beside Helena.

"My name was Thomas," he says quietly. He is lanky, with reddish hair. "For me it was the late 1700s, America. Just call me Tom."

"Thomas…?" Hank leans closer as if trying to get a better look, to figure something out. "What was your last name?"

Tom looks down shyly. "Jefferson."

"The President?" Hank asks.

Tom meets his eyes, his cheeks red as he nods.

"Unbelievable!" Hank is practically bouncing as he takes Tom's hand and shakes it up and down. "My name is Hank," he says, "and I lived in America too, in the early 1800s. I learned all about you. Once I rode all night, fifty miles, just to see you speak. The Sieve showed it to me. This is amazing. I can't believe it!"

"I know," Tom demurs.

The few memories that the Sieve has shown me didn't reveal anything about a president named Thomas Jefferson, but I do remember enough to know that being the president is a big deal.

"I'm an American, too," I say. "That makes three of us. But I lived much later, probably in the 2000s."

"2000s?" Pierre says. "That's the latest date I've ever heard. What was your name?"

"Paul Fitzroy. I was a doctor. You can call me Cipher."

185

The girl beside me goes next. She reminds of me of Kiyo, with straight black hair and dark eyes. She says that she lived in Japan in the 1600s, and that her father was a leading shogun. Her name is Hama Tokugawa.

Next is Shelley. She tells the group that I'd somehow inspired her to use more of her power over the air. She couldn't move anything big, of course, but she said that together with me, she'd managed to capture two in the Scouring. "Oh, and before this place," she adds, "I was English. Mary Shelley. A writer in the 1800s."

"You…Frankenstein?" Tom asks in awe.

Shelley nods, her eyes studying the floor.

"Not bad," Pierre says. "A writer, a preacher, a president, a doctor, and an emperor's mom. Who's next?"

The rest of the group follows in order, giving a name, a time, and a place. The overlaps between us are too much to be coincidence. There are three Americans, three Japanese, three English, two Romans, and Pierre from France. A few were famous, like Helena, Tom, and Shelley, but the rest of us seem normal. It's hard to see any other pattern. Maybe we had some kind of similar life experience despite our differences—based on my story, I figure it's missing fathers, overactive minds, or brilliant egos. Probably all of the above, but no one likes to admit that.

# 45

PIERRE TAKES THE lead again after everyone has introduced themselves. He tells us we need to agree on a plan, and he points down at the large map in front of him, finger landing in the middle of the mountains beyond the red tower. "I say we go for Red."

"Seriously?" Tom asks. "Red?"

Pierre nods. "They're our natural enemy, and I've seen the last two winning groups steal from them. We're going to do it the same way."

"What way is that?" Tom asks. "Listen, I spent time in Red. We don't want to mess with them."

"Why?" I ask, fascinated that Tom remembers it.

"Where to begin?" He shakes his head. "For starters, the mountains are almost impassable. The peaks are covered with snow, and almost no one ever goes to the coast. It's too cold. They stay near their fires, in the tower. But even if we did find someone, the girls can *make* fire, and the boys fight hard. Together they can control the fire to a point. They'll burn us up if they find us. It's a fierce place."

"Maybe it is," Pierre says, "but I'm telling you, other teams from Blue have done it. You can't argue with that. And we all know Red can't control themselves. We just have to find a way to lure someone out. Probably one of the boys. I heard the last group sent a girl on her own into the mountains, while the other eleven stayed hidden and watched. The girl was pretty." Pierre turns to Helena. "Red boys can't resist that."

"You want to use me as bait?" Helena asks.

"Yes."

She laughs uneasily. "At least my talents are appreciated..."

"We won't let you be taken," Pierre says. "We'll stay close."

"You don't think Red has figured it out?" Tom asks. "Apparently this happened to them twice recently. They may not be geniuses, but they're not idiots."

"Tom has a point," Hank leans over the map. "What else has worked? Which other color should we target?"

"I've seen this more than any of you." Pierre takes a step toward Hank. "Are you trying to lead?"

"No." Hank stands his ground. "I'm saying Cipher should lead."

"That little boy?" Pierre laughs as he looks down at me. "You can't be serious."

"He's different," Hank says. "No one has ever advanced as fast as he has. And he has gifts, I've seen it."

"Like what?"

"He controls more air than anyone." Hank glances around the group. "Way more. He blew a boy out of his desk and across the classroom...in his first class."

Pierre turns to me. "Is that true? Show me."

I hesitate. I glance to the side at Emma. She has been watching all this quietly. Now she nods. I turn back to Pierre and summon just enough of a breeze to pick up the map we've been staring at and blow it into his face.

He tries to pull it off, while others start to laugh.

I finally let go of the wind. The paper falls.

In an instant Pierre is in front of me. "Don't do that again."

Helena laughs like it's all a big joke. "I still think Pierre should lead us. He's stronger, with more experience."

"Let's put it to a vote," Hank suggests.

"What's your plan?" Tom asks me quietly. It's hard to believe he was a president, and now a Red tower survivor.

Again all eyes fall on me. I don't have a plan, but as I look at Helena I remember how she'd captured Jack from the Green tower. It seems like we'd have a better chance there, but maybe we could use Pierre's idea.

"I've sailed to Yellow's land, and just past that is Green," I say. "We all know they are hunters. They probably go off alone in their forest beyond their tower. I say we go there and pluck off one of them who is wandering near the sea. Maybe we could lure one out like Pierre said, if we need to."

"Cipher's right," Hank says. "I know. I've been Green."

"Really?" He'd left that out of his story.

"I got wiped when I came here, but I've seen a couple things in the Sieve." Hank glances down at the map that has fallen to the floor. "The forest is a wild place, but at least the girls there can't fling fireballs at us. And the boys do go off hunting alone sometimes."

"Bad idea," Pierre snaps. "Green might be wild, but they

189

stay in packs, like a bunch of wolves. It's also harder to get to Green. They have scouts. They'll see us coming. With all the mountains around Red, we can get in undetected. We can send out Helena and stay close, watching until the trap is ready."

"I *am* enticing," Helena says, looking around the group. "So why don't we vote already? You've all heard the ideas. All in favor of Pierre, like me, raise your hands."

A few hands go up, then more, making five total.

"And all in favor of Cipher?"

Seven hands, including mine.

Hank grabs my raised hand like I'm a prize fighter. "Seven to five. We're going to capture someone from Green.

# 46

A HEAVY MIST shrouds the sea and a falcon soars above as we board our boat the next morning. The boat is the same kind as the one we used during my first boat race, but larger, with lines of oars on each side and a tall mast. The twelve members of our group are dressed in the blue robes of third and fourth class, with our hoods up for warmth. We look almost identical despite our varied pasts. Our twelve servants are dressed in white robes, with silver links at their necks. I have no clue about the servants' pasts, except for Emma's. While we were planning the day before, I asked the three servants from the Green tower as much as I could about where we should dock our boat, and where people might be hunting. They confirmed it's not going to be easy.

The servants start at the oars, filling all twelve spots on the benches on either side of the boat. We unfurl the sail, and I keep it taut by channeling a steady wind at our backs. I'm stronger now. It's faster progress than when Emma and I sailed alone in our little boat to Yellow.

Without storms and with a good wind, we spend only three nights on board before we see the first trees of green along the coast. It has gone from steep rock cliffs to rolling yellow fields to forest. The trees look like a wall in the distance. Not gradual, but immediate and huge and impenetrable.

"How should we dock?" Hank asks, standing beside me at the bow of the boat. He has stayed close to me for most of the voyage. He's like a first mate.

The Green shore looks like a dense tangle of mangroves growing out into the water. It has no sandy beaches, coves, or piers where we can leave the boat.

"Let's anchor at a safe distance," I say, "We can send in a first group to scout things out."

Hank nods. "Good plan. How many should go?"

"Ten. I'll go with Emma. You, Pierre, and Tom should come, too, with your servants."

"And maybe Helena?"

I groan. "Why?"

"I know she can be annoying, but she does have a way with boys. And her servant, Jack, could be an asset in these woods."

I reluctantly agree, because I know he's right, and we start organizing our group. We don't have any smaller boats to take to the shore. There's a chance I could form a platform of air to carry us all over the water, but that would sap my energy. Better save some for the forest. For Green.

So we swim. We strip off our heavy robes and jump into the water in our undergarments. Helena's servant carries a pack of supplies and our bundled-up robes—which I wrap in a bubble of air to keep dry—as he swims. In all our time at sea, Helena has made Jack do a hundred things like this, and yet he's never complained. His expression stays blank as his strong frame does the work. I can't shake the thought that there's some kind of rage lurking underneath.

As we make our way to the mangroves, I think of when I first entered the Blue Tower, swimming like this, with no idea of where I was. Would newcomers to Green start in the middle of the forest? That seems easier, because you can't drown in a forest.

When we finally reach the mangroves, it's even harder going. Their roots divide and spread into the water like dense nets. They're not alive. Not grabbing at our legs and ankles. But it sure feels like it. We have to fight for every step, moving slowly, deliberately, through the swamp. By the time our feet reach solid ground, our boat can no longer be seen through the mangroves. We put on our robes and trudge on.

The forest is even denser than I expected, with ferns and other bushes hiding the ground and trees reaching up like iron fingers. We need some way to find our way back, without being so obvious that anyone from Green could follow the trail to us. Jack says he knows how to read broken branches and footsteps to guide us back. I don't want to rely on him, but it's better than dropping breadcrumbs. I agree to the plan, and whisper to Emma—who stays back with the servants—that she should keep a constant eye on him.

Helena is not happy about our progress. She looks tired and angry, like an Imperatrix, whatever that is. Her thick brown hair is still wet. "How far are we planning to march in like hippos?" she asks. "Anyone from Green will hear us coming."

"You have a better idea?"

"Yes. This." Her hands clasp in front of her, as if

pleading, and her bottom lip begins to quiver. "Please…help me…I'm lost…"

I see what she's doing. She still wants to be bait, and she's good at it. Her big dark eyes, on the verge of tears, are as disarming as a puppy's. "Okay, it might work. But what if a girl finds you first?"

"You'll be close behind, right? I'll shout if I need help."

It seems like a better idea than a group of us bustling through these foreign woods with a hope that we'll stumble upon someone from Green. "What do the rest of you think?" I ask the group.

Pierre says he's with Helena. Emma gives me a little nod. Hank shrugs.

"The rest of us will have to stay together," Tom says. "But still…what if they capture Helena, she'll tell them about us, and then we're live meat for hunting?"

"That won't happen," Helena says. "I know how to perform."

Tom is right. Part of me worries about Helena. "You could be caught without us noticing."

"So? The rest of you can do your best to get away."

"Do you want to go Green or something?" Hank asks.

"I want to win," Helena says. "Just stay close. I won't get caught quietly."

"Alright," I say, catching Jack's wild eyes. "We'll be close."

# 47

THE GREEN TOWER'S forest is the worst. Branches and thorns batter me while I bat at bugs. Each step in, stumbling one root at a time, seems to make it darker and sweatier. At first the robes were the problem. The heavy, loose cloth is like a parachute, getting caught behind with every move forward. I was the first to strip out of it and tie it to my back. So now I'm down to my underwear—a mosquito magnet of pale flesh masquerading through the dense trees, ready with my blood to offer.

It is impossible to keep track of time. Even though Green has sun like Yellow, it can't shine through the dense canopy to the bottom of the forest. The terrain has been gently rising since we waded through the mangroves by the shore. The trees block the view of what's ahead, but my legs feel the effort of a steady incline. The sounds have been mostly the same. Insects chirping and birds chattering. Sometimes I feel like they're laughing at me. I never would have believed how loud they can be.

We stop to eat whenever Helena stops. We trade out the lead watcher. Someone stays ahead of our group, halfway between us and Helena. That person's job is to keep an eye on her and report if anything happens.

I'm on my second turn as lead watcher when a low, rumbling sound rises in the distance. I try to keep an eye on Helena, but some verdant branch is constantly swiping at my eyes. The foliage is so dense that I can hardly see her, and only then because she's out of her robe and down to her undergarments. The white cloth is easier to see than her robe. For me and the mosquitoes.

Then I glimpse a streak of white through the trees. A waterfall. As I move closer to it, tracking Helena, I see that it's at least a hundred feet high, taller than most of the trees. The water streams off a rock cliff that juts out of the land. Trees and vines cling to the cliff face, so that it looks like a green, living wall. My eyes follow the long white stream down to a large, still pool of water. Helena stands at the edge.

She steps into the water and swims towards the pool's center. I'm suddenly jealous. The water must feel good. I imagine its coolness washing over my millions of red welts gifted by the bugs.

"Whoa!" a voice whispers behind me.

It's Hank and the rest of the group close behind. I was so lost in my own wonder at the waterfall that I'd forgotten they would catch up to me once I stopped.

"Shhh." I point to the pool. "She swam out there. I'm not sure how we're supposed to get past this wall."

"Who's that?" Emma asks quietly, pointing past me.

I follow her outstretched arm to the opposite side of the pool. My breath freezes as I see a dark figure, silhouetted by the dense spray of the waterfall. The person slowly backs away, disappearing behind the mist.

196

# 48

"WE SHOULD RUN." Hank is pulling at my sleeve. "He's going to get others. They'll know we're here now."

"No, we can't leave Helena," I say. "Maybe he only saw her and won't know we're here. If she draws more of them out, we can catch one and then go."

"That's bold." Pierre comes to my other side, eyeing the waterfall ahead. "I'd rather not wait to find out how many people are coming. We have to get back to the rest of our group."

"I agree, but Cipher's right," Hank says. "We have to get Helena first."

"I'll go." Emma steps forward, and no one objects as she heads toward the pool, probably because she's the only other girl in our group, and she's quiet.

"Everyone else be on your guard," I say. Not that there's much they need to do. We packed light and haven't set up camp. Tom is already edging his way back the way we came, looking around us into the trees.

I creep ahead twenty paces, following Emma, then stop behind a tree to watch. There's no sign of anyone where the dark figure had appeared in the mist.

Emma reaches the edge of the pool. She's far enough away—and the waterfall is loud enough—that I can't hear whatever she says to Helena.

But Helena turns with a look of surprise. Emma motions for her to come, holding out the robe for Helena to slide on.

A noise makes me turn to glance back at our group. They are standing motionless, looking away from me, at Tom. I see a glint of light at his neck.

A dagger.

The boy behind Tom looks straight at me. "Hands up," he says. "Join your friends."

They moved fast. It's not like I can run anywhere, so I do what he says. Tom looks terrified. The boy has him held tight, lean muscles in his arms flexed, the sharp metal pressed against Tom's neck.

"What do you want?" I ask, considering grabbing the boy's arm with the air. I'm not sure I can be quick enough to stop him.

The boy nods past me. "Her."

Helena and Emma are in sight, moving toward us. Their casual stride suggests they haven't seen what's happening. I'm tempted to yell, *run!*, but I can't risk Tom.

"You give me the girl," the boy says, "and I'll let you go." He's wearing only a loincloth made from hide and his brown skin is caked in mud. It's primitive, savage, but he sounds reasonable. Except it's not a fair deal. I can't give up Helena just to walk away empty-handed.

"You're surrounded," the boy adds. "Fifty of us."

No one is visible among the trees.

The boy seems to sense my doubt. He whistles three

times, sounding like a bird. Another boy emerges from the trees, invisible one moment, and standing before us wielding a spear the next moment. It's Jack.

"Jack, Jack…" Helena says as she joins us, looking from her servant to the newcomer. "What's your friend's name?"

Jack smiles wide. "He's Jones. My brother."

*Brother?* I think. *How does anyone have a brother here?*

"He's even more handsome than you are," Helena says as she casually lifts her hand and dangles her fingers like a puppet master. I can guess what she's thinking—Jack has to do whatever she says as long as the link is around his neck.

"So what is it?" Jack's brother asks. "We take the girl, and we let you leave?"

"You can have her, and your brother," I say. "But you have to give us someone in exchange."

A few gasps come from our group. It's risky, but as long as Helena can control Jack, we have the upper hand. Besides, nothing in the rules of the game says we have to come back with our full group.

"Deal." The boy whistles again, with a string of notes too complex for me to follow.

The man who emerges next from the woods is nothing like the others. He leans over on a gnarled staff, looking more ancient than the towering trees above. His beard is as long as Abram's.

"This is Dan," the boy says. "He has agreed to go with you."

The old man stands still while Jack and his brother move slowly toward us. Helena and Emma are beside each other. This should work. Jack's brother will let go of Tom and take

Helena. Then we take the old man and we're gone.

Once Jack and his brother are within reach of Helena, they go perfectly still. Everyone is motionless, waiting.

"Let him go," I say. "Take the girl."

Jones glances at Jack, who gives two quick whistles. They move suddenly, in perfect unison, as Jack grabs Tom and his brother shoves Helena to the ground. Before I can even react, Jones has Emma in his arms, knife at her throat.

# 49

"NO!" I SHOUT, as Jack's brother, Jones, backs away with Emma. "Not that girl."

"You didn't specify," Jack says, grinning. "We choose this one."

It's a stupid trick. I can't let them take Emma. I meet her eyes, as a beam of light finds its way through the canopy above and reflects against the dagger and silver link at her neck. She doesn't look as afraid as she should. Maybe that's because of what she sees in my eyes.

"Let her go," I demand.

The boy whistles again, like he's giving orders. "Take Dan and leave," he says. "Or people are going to get hurt."

"Wrong," Helena says, rising to her feet and meeting my eyes. "Show them, Cipher."

I nod. She can stop Jack through their link. I can handle Jones and the others. Good thing I saved some energy.

Time seems to stand still as I weave the power. I gather the air around Emma, careful not to let it touch the Green boy—not yet. I pull next on Emma's power, weaving the streams of healing yellow with the blue of the wind. I make a seamless web of air, ready to drop between our groups, while at the same time I form a razor-thin, invisible rope and wrap it slowly around Jones's wrist and dagger.

"Now!" In one quick movement, I set it all in motion. I yank the boy's arm away from Emma's neck and throw him down to the ground. His eyes open wide in shock, and Emma dashes forward. Then I let the web drop, with the old man, Jack, and Tom inside.

Everyone springs into motion. The boys from Green begin throwing spears at us. I see Helena's servant Jack lift one but drop it, his hands going to the silver band at his neck. The other spears fly at us from every direction but stop and fall midair when they slam against my wall. Each hit feels like a slap in the face, but my fear and anger give me more power than I've ever used before. The wall around us holds.

Emma pulls me away, to follow after our fleeing group. It takes all my energy to keep the wall up, moving it with us as we move, and as Green keeps up the assault. We run, stumbling through the forest with the ferns and other plants grabbing at us as we race past. I feel weak, covered in sweat. My mind begins to cave in more with every attack.

In that moment of concentration, a memory comes to me from the Sieve: surgery. My hands wield the scalpel, carving into someone, where the slightest lapse could be lethal. I work while others talk around me. My hands and my mind melded, nothing able to shift my focus. I feel the same way now. I feel like I'm doing exactly what I was born to do—protecting, saving.

"Come on!" Hank shouts. He is waist-deep in the water, holding out his arms to me.

I hadn't even noticed that we'd reached the shore. The others manage to grab me and help me through the mangroves.

There is shouting all around as we begin to swim away from the shore. The group from the Green tower stands among the dense trees, watching us leave, hurling more weapons at us. I almost sink a dozen times, but with the others' help I keep the wall up until we're out of range. I slip briefly out of consciousness, only to startle back awake when ropes are dropping beside us. Hank and Jack are keeping me afloat as they tie the rope around me.

"Try to hold on," Hank says as I'm hauled up and onto the boat.

I fall onto my back, staring up at the sky. A ring of faces surrounds me.

"What happened?"

"You caught one?"

"Are you okay?"

"He'll be fine," Emma says softly, kneeling beside me and cradling my head.

# 50

THE OLD MAN from the Green Tower doesn't say a single word on our return voyage. We all take turns trying to get him to speak. Three days, three nights, a thousand questions. Nothing.

As soon as he set foot on the boat, he shuffled to the bow and pointed to the horizon, in the direction we were planning to go. I asked him why he was pointing. He took hold of my hand and studied the scar, but he didn't answer. I told him he was our captive and we were taking him to Blue. He didn't react. I asked him if he was going to try to run away. He just smiled, shaking his head slightly. At least it was a response.

He stayed rooted to the same spot the whole journey back. He didn't even move when the rain poured one night. After that he looked like a little old mushroom draped in glistening wet moss. We caught him sleeping a few times, but just for short stints, and sitting upright. I'd never seen anything like it.

The only eventful thing on the boat happened the first night, as Emma and I ate salted fish and watched a sunset beyond Yellow's territory. The light reflected over the steady rising and falling of ocean waves, an ever-changing blur of yellow and blue so beautifully complex that I could watch it forever.

"You were lucky in Yellow, to have sun," I said to Emma.

"I am lucky to have the Healer," she replied, her face and hair gold in the day's fading light. "But Yellow has given me up."

"You still want to go back?" I asked.

She took my hand in hers, running her slender fingers over the scar. She looked concentrated, then frustrated. "I still can't heal this. It is not even like a wound. It's…part of you now."

"Guess the Blue Tower left its mark."

She met my eyes, and her words surprised me. "I want to convert."

"To Blue?"

"To Blue. I want to look in the Sieve."

"But you said you've seen your past. Why would you need the Sieve?"

"The Sieve sounds different, like it shows the most important things. It has made you different. I'm ready."

Two days later, when we've left any trace of the sun behind and the old man from Green is still rooted like a silent tree on the bow of our boat, we reach the Blue Tower. Some of our group ties the boat to the dock. Pierre, Hank, and I go to the old man, the captive. We're ready to drag him off the boat if we have to.

"This is the Blue Tower," I say to him. "You're coming inside with us."

The man stands slowly and looks at all of us and winks.

Then he disappears. Vanishes completely.

"Hey-o!" the shout makes all of us turn. And there's the

old man, standing on the dock, leaning on his stick. I would swear he's smiling, but we can't see his mouth through the thick beard. He waves toward the tower, where we see Abram approaching.

Abram walks straight to the old man. "Daniel! Why have you come, my friend?"

The answer that comes out of the man's lips sounds deep as a wolf's growl, but I can make out the words. So he *can* speak.

"You have the one," he says. "The final one."

"We all do."

The man clasps Abram's arm. "It is so good to see you. Been too long. We must palaver."

"Yes, yes." Abram turns with him and they head toward the tower.

"Wait!" I shout, running after them. "We completed the Hunting. What's our reward?"

Abram smiles at me. "You have done well." He looks past me and motions for everyone from our boat to gather around. "No one from your group will be reset. How'd you do it?"

"Cipher got us out of the Green forest alive, and brought that…man," Hank says. "He deserves promotion."

"I see." Abram turns to Pierre. "What do the rest of you think?"

Pierre shrugs. "Yeah, he probably deserves it."

"He offered to trade me," Helena says. "He was going to let Green take me."

"Did they?" Abram sounds amused.

Helena meets Abram's gaze, defiant. "No, but…it was

close."

"Were any of you harmed?" Abram asks.

"My arm was cut pretty bad." Tom's voice is quiet as he looks to Emma. "But I'm okay now. Emma healed me."

"Thank you for helping Blue, Emma," Abram says. "You know the Healer well. Tell me, what have you learned of the Genius?"

"You were right," Emma replies. "A facet of the same jewel. And if Cipher represents the Genius, then it is a logical and powerful facet. That's why I'm ready to convert."

Abram studies Emma, then turns to me. "You believe she is ready?"

I do not hesitate. "Yes."

"About time!" Hank says. "If the whole point of this is to make us stronger for the Scouring, we want Cipher at his best." He crosses his strong arms across his chest. "I won't go to the Scouring again without him. So Emma converts. Cipher makes fourth class. Blue keeps winning."

"I will consider it. Emma should rest now." Abram motions to me. "You will join us."

I move slowly to him, feeling like a student who has just been called to the principal's office. And for what? For leading a successful journey? As Abram turns to go, Daniel gives me a wink, but this time he doesn't disappear. I trail behind them as we make our way into the tower.

# 51

THE TWO WHITE-bearded men lead me up the winding incline to the top of the Blue Tower, step by shuffling step. When we finally reach the familiar wooden door, Abram makes way for the old man from Green. I follow them inside.

The Sieve sits silently, as if beckoning, in the middle of the room. By the wall of glass overlooking the Scouring, three chairs sit in a perfect triangle on a thick carpet that has an ornate pattern of interlocking circles—like yin-yangs but far more complex as they are made of five colors instead of two—blue, yellow, green, red, and black. I'm sure that neither the chairs nor the carpet was here before. As I take the open seat, I notice that in the center of the carpet, between our three chairs, there's a white circle.

"You want him to hear this?" Daniel asks.

"I'm afraid he must. It is earlier than I would like, but he is almost ready." Abram speaks as if I'm not in the room. "We can talk freely, only not of the greatest thing."

"Yes, of course." Daniel's eyebrows are impossibly thick. It's a strange thing to notice at a time like this. But they are like two inches of gray wool bushing out from his leathery skin. "You know the latest count?"

Abram nods somberly. "Blue rises, but Black does not fall."

"They are too powerful," Daniel says. "I'm afraid Green has fallen to last, and Red falls even faster."

"Red will need help. Blue will be in balance soon."

"Only because you have him." Now Daniel is looking at me, speaking about me as if I'm not even there. "I saw the scar on his hand. You know what this means. The end is near."

"My friend, have we been here so long that we accept such imprecision?" Abram asks. "It is no end, not at all. It is only the completion of this place. The beginning, really."

"I know, I know." Daniel leans back in his chair, hands on his knees. "But you see where I am heading. How many more Scourings will it take?"

"Five, ten, a thousand...." Abram says. "Does it matter?"

"Even I can grow tired."

"Come now, don't tell me your hope dims."

"No, heavens no." Daniel laughs. "The light can't dim, but can't an old man feel tired? We all felt tired sometimes on earth."

"This is not earth, my friend."

I have been holding my tongue, following their exchange, fascinated. But this is too much. "If it's not earth, what is it?"

They both turn to me, like wizards amused by their pupil. There is tenderness in their eyes, but pain too. Daniel is right. They both look very old, and very tired.

"We are in between, Cipher. But you already knew that." Abram points to the Sieve. "You've seen what was before."

"But not what's next," I say. "We're between earth and

what?"

The old men exchange a glance, smiling like old friends sharing an inside joke. Abram holds his large, weathered hand out to Daniel, as if suggesting he answer this one. I wonder what kind of man Abram was when younger, to have had such strong hands.

Daniel's calculating eyes look at me from under the gray canopy of eyebrows. "What's the best thing you can imagine?"

I'm stumped. Without more memories, without earth, I find it hard to imagine the *best thing*. I imagine towers and a broken past. But there was something in the memory of my Mom. Something in Kiyo's and Emma's stories. Traces of a common thread, weaving through them all, lead to my guess: "A place full of love?"

"Not bad!" Daniel says. "That is part of it."

"How do I get there?" I ask.

"Daniel and I are only stewards," Abram says. "We ensure the process works fairly, because we understand its purpose. But not even we know how long it takes, how it works, or what's next. Time is different here, as you have seen. But it still moves forward in a way, and we cannot see the future."

"What is the process?"

"The Scouring," Daniel says, turning to Abram. "Do you tell them nothing in Blue?"

Abram shrugs. "We receive the most gifted minds. They do not lack for intellect or reason, but this brings its own unique variety of pride. More knowledge makes it worse."

"You really should try other towers soon," Daniel says to

me. "In Green we are honest about this as soon as a newcomer arrives. You must be scoured of mortal sins. It's the same for everyone here." He glances at Abram, as if expecting to be chastised for saying too much.

But Abram only nods. "In Blue we use the Sieve. Others are different, as you may learn. But there's more you need to see here. I'd like Daniel to watch this time. Are you ready?"

I follow Abram's gaze to the pedestal of water. The cool stone is not inviting, and the last memory that I saw in it makes me hesitate. My memories are painful but, somehow, irresistible. Abram was right—I can't stand not knowing, especially about myself.

"Okay," I say.

The men stand slowly, and we walk together to the Sieve. Just above the glassy surface, I can see my reflection. Compared to the old men, I look so young, so innocent. I'm beginning to understand. I'm ready to face my past self again.

# 52

I'M DRIVING THROUGH a neighborhood. Stately oak trees and brick mansions line the road. They pass in a blur. My foot presses down on the pedal, and I know why. I'm late, very late, for my son's birthday. The classical music—Bach, I remember—does little to soothe my nerves.

I brake hard and make a sharp left turn into a driveway. A wrought iron gate, with the letter F in its center, swings open. The driveway leads to a mansion. My house.

It's staggering, bigger than anyone could ever need. I feel shame as I think of how it compares to where I lived as a child, in my last memory. This house is big enough for a village to live inside.

I park in the five-car garage and enter the home through the side door into the kitchen. Sunlight spills through the huge windows at the back, and a loud chorus fills the air—a chorus of children's voices. I follow the sound, passing through a hallway with pictures along the wall.

One picture makes me freeze. It's Mom kneeling beside me as a kid, not much older than in the last memory that the Sieve showed me. Seeing this makes me know: she died when I was young.

I begin moving again, to a dining room where dozens are gathered around a double-decker cake on a table. Six candles. Smoke still drifting up.

The boy behind them sees me. He runs to me smiling, as if I could ever deserve the joy that my arrival brings him. His innocent eyes look up from under a mop of brown hair. His grandmother's eyes.

"You're here," he says.

I pull him into a hug. "Better late than never. Happy birthday, bud."

"Thanks!" He turns back to his friends, who have started on the cake. Their laughing mouths are covered in white icing.

I glance around the crowd, seeing familiar faces. I'm aware of this place, but also of the reality through the Sieve. As I step forward and join the conversation, a hand on my shoulder makes me turn.

My wife. Her calm brown eyes make the memories fall on me like a stack of bricks. Her name was Susan. She looks hurt but unflappable, like a woman of infinite patience and light squaring off against a black hole.

"I'm surprised you made it," she says, folding her arms across her chest. She wears a plain green sweater and a gold necklace with a shape hanging from it—two straight, perpendicular lines—matching the new scar on my hand. "Work again?"

I'm nodding, telling her some excuse that she and I both know is not entirely true. I could have been here. It just wasn't important enough.

Someone joins us. A man I can't remember.

"Dr. Fitzroy?" he asks.

213

"That's me."

He holds out his hand. "Sam Connors. It's a real honor to meet you. You operated on my daughter last year. You saved her life."

A smile spreads across my face. Dr. Fitzroy's thoughts, my thoughts, spill over me like black ink. Mr. Connors makes me feel superior, as if he somehow owes me this gratitude, that he and his daughter should feel lucky to have had my brilliance touch their lives.

I realize some of the things I should have said: *It's a pleasure to meet you. How is she now? I did only what I could.* But instead the words out of my lips are: "I remember. Hard case, cranial fusion. Good thing I was available."

Sam's face retreats into something like surprise and indignity. He says a few words of thanks and walks off.

My wife grabs my arm and pulls me into the hallway. She is staring at me with a touch of horror. "I can't believe you said that."

"What?"

She shakes her head. "You used to at least pretend to care." Her words are quiet, barely audible above the noise of the kids' talking in the next room, but filling my mind and resounding through it.

"I'm here, aren't I?" Hearing this makes me cringe at my own words. I want to reach into the memory and make myself shut up, but I'm forced to watch, helpless.

"Only so you can look good as a dad," she snaps. "You're becoming no better than your own father." She spins off, and as the vision begins to recede, going black, I know she's right. My father was never there.

# 53

THE GLASS WALLS atop the Blue Tower surround me. Cool stone floor at my back. The mansion, the wife, the son—they're all gone. The Sieve stands lifeless beside me.

Abram's face comes into view. "Need a hand?"

I take his hand and rise slowly to my feet.

"You've been out a long time," he says.

It's dark outside the glass room. I feel like I've run a thousand miles. My legs shake as I stand.

"It's awful," I say. "The memories."

"Everyone wishes they'd done better. Everyone makes mistakes. Not everyone gets a chance to be scoured."

"Why do I get the chance?"

"Because you were saved."

"But how?"

Abram smiles. "Get to the White Tower. Then you'll know."

"How do I get in?"

"Daniel and I told you. Everyone must be scoured, completely."

I look around the room and realize for the first time that Daniel is gone. "Where did he go?"

"He had to visit another leader."

"I don't understand."

"He saw your mother in that picture, and he recognized her. He wanted to share what he learned."

"He recognized her?" My knees feel weak. "You don't mean…she's here?"

"Yes."

My throat constricts, like a fist has grabbed it. "And my wife? My son?"

Abram shakes his head. "Not all need to be scoured as you do."

"Are they alive?"

"More alive than you. You'll see in the White Tower."

His answer annoys me. I'm tired of hearing about the White Tower, about scouring. It's torture to make me see these things from my past but keep them out of my reach, like a carrot on a stick. But Mom is here. Maybe she's reachable. Maybe I can help her. "Where's my Mom?"

"That's not for me to say."

"Where!"

"I can't."

This time the answer pushes me over the edge. Without thinking about what I'm doing, I'm summoning the air, as much as I can draw, and I coil it around Abram and lift him off the ground. I rotate him until he is parallel to the ground, his face in front of mine.

"Tell me," I growl. "Now."

"You are more powerful than they said." Abram's voice is perfectly calm, even as his body hovers, suspended in air. "I will tell you what I can. Daniel left for the Red Tower."

The quiet calm of Abram's voice suddenly makes me ashamed. I slowly unwind the air and lower him to his feet. "I'm sorry."

"It's okay. Unsurprising, really. This is why you're here."

His patient eyes, like calm lakes, deepen my shame. I look away and mutter, "I understand."

"You've seen enough of your memory to know that darker spots remain. More must be brought to light."

"Why…?" I begin, but I know. I cover my face with my hands as I feel the heat of tears. He is right. All these things in me, from before, are bad. Very bad. Everything in the memory had seemed so perfect—my career, my home, my family. But I was a wreck in the middle of a mansion.

Abram puts his hand on my shoulder. "The Sieve has done what was needed. You are ready to find your own way now. Other towers will need your help, and you will need them."

I lower my hands. Abram's bearded face looks blurry through my tears. "You mean I can leave?"

"You may," he says. "Many stay in the same tower, needing only one facet of the jewel to be purified. Others may need two towers, or three. A few people require all five towers. The Scouring, the Hunting, the captures—all serve this purpose in time. But it is rare indeed for anyone to move towers by choice, facing the risk of losing what memories they've gained."

"I see."

"It's up to you," Abram says. "I will bring Emma for the initiation now. Once that is done, you may leave. There will be a Scouring tomorrow. You will lead a team of your choosing, and you will be free to chart your own course, knowing that more cleansing lies ahead."

As he walks to the door, the memory of my Mom's face rushes back to me. She is here, maybe without memories, maybe trapped in the Red Tower. That is where I must go.

# 54

"WHO SPONSORS THIS initiate?" Abram asks, standing beside Emma and me, with a hand on the rim of the Sieve.

"I do," I say.

"Then you must look together." Abram's expression is solemn. "If you still believe she is ready for initiation after what you see, then she enters. If not, she resets. You know some of her past?" Abram asks me.

"Yes."

"This will be more," he says, stepping to the side. "Much more. Come, hold her hand as she looks."

I take Emma's hand and we move forward to the Sieve. The reflection of her hair on the Sieve's water is like a shooting gold star across a midnight sky.

"I'm ready," she says, turning to me. "I hope you're ready to forgive."

"It's the past," I say. "There's nothing to forgive."

"There will be."

She squeezes my hand, takes a deep breath, and plunges her face into the dark water.

The tiny room has cracked plaster walls and a dirt floor.

There is a single bed, a small table with two chairs, and a fire burning in the hearth. It barely keeps the room warm. A man lays on the bed, covered in blankets, eyes closed. His face is so chalk white and thin that I'd think it was a skull if not for the swoop of brown curly hair matted to his forehead.

Emma sits beside the man. She is a young woman, even more beautiful than I imagined she'd be. But pain and fatigue weigh on her eyes. It looks like she hasn't slept in weeks. A heavy sigh escapes her delicate lips as she dips a cloth into a bucket of water by her feet and gently wipes the man's face.

Then a muffled sound comes from Emma's chest. A bundle is tied there, and as the sound rises to cries, I realize it is a baby.

"Shhh, shhh." She stands, swaying gently.

But the cries rise louder and louder. They echo around the bare room as Emma moves to one of the hard wooden chairs and begins to nurse the infant. She looks into the baby's face with the fullest expression a person can have—heartache, exhaustion, and deep unconditional love.

The man's eyes begin to blink open. He lays there in silence, watching Emma as she nurses the baby, unaware of his gaze. She quietly sings a song while the baby feeds, the beauty of her voice wholly out of place in the squalor:

*The water is wide, I cannot cross o'er*
*And neither have I wings to fly*
*Give me a boat that can carry two*
*And both shall row, my child and I...*

When the baby finishes, she stands, gently patting it on the back. She notices the man watching her for the first time.

"John," she whispers.

"I am here," he says, his voice faint and cracked.

She smiles briefly, but then the look of pain returns. She wraps the baby again to her chest, within the cloth wrapping around her body, and she moves to the man's side and leans forward so he can see the baby's face. "Your son is growing stronger."

"Good, very good." The man's eyes close again.

Emma leans back in her chair and quietly begins to cry. Through the day, the night, and the next day she steadily tends to the man, who never once rises and only looks worse and worse. She nurses the baby, changes his clothes. She goes outside, pulling a worn shawl tight around her. She gets wood for the fire and feeds a cow and three chickens. She tries many times to lift a ladle to the man's mouth and pour a few drops of water in, but it only runs down his chin. She sleeps an hour or two while the baby does, sitting at the foot of the bed with her head leaned against the wall.

On the third evening, the man dies.

Emma weeps so hard that her body shudders. Her son wails with her. The dirge continues through the night, but as the first light shines through the room's single window, Emma goes silent. She steps to the door, opens it slowly, and looks to the rising sun. The sky is majestic, orange and lavender painting huge clouds that seem to explode out of the horizon.

Emma's head tilts down to her son, and her expression turns from pain to love to resolve. She goes back into the room and gathers her things into a small bag. Then she walks away from her dead husband and the poor hovel and the farm.

*This is different.*

I'm shocked to hear the words in my mind. It is Emma's voice, but not the Emma that I see, walking over the crest of a hill through the countryside, clutching her baby tight.

*This is me, walking toward my family's manor,* Emma says, her voice both sad and confused. *But I could never bring myself to do this, to return home. I'd told my father I would never come back. I'd sworn he'd never see my face. So I'd stayed, and it ended for me as it did for John.*

*This is different.*

Emma and her baby trek for several days. Her pace slows but never stops. She manages to find rides from two separate farmers who offer to let her lie in their wagons. The resolve never slips from Emma's face.

On the fourth day since her husband died, she turns from the road through a hedgerow gate. A man by the gate approaches her. "Emma?" he asks. "It can't be…"

"It's me," she says. "Tell my father."

The man runs off towards a huge manor in the distance. Emma seems frozen where she stands in the gate, as if unable to take another step forward. She cowers back as a figure appears on a horse in the distance. The figure rides toward her at a full gallop.

The man on horseback is stunning as he draws closer. He rides with vigor, his gaze unwavering and eager. He wears a thick red robe and has long blond hair. As blond as Emma's.

He leaps from the horse once he reaches her. Still she cowers back.

"I'm sorry," she says.

But he hardly seems to hear her. He's engulfing her in a

hug. He's crying with joy. "Oh Emma, Emma! You've come back home! Thank the Lord, you've come back."

A sound between them makes the man peel away. "Who's this?" he asks, a radiant smile filling his handsome face.

"My son, Oliver."

"My grandson! Oh, Emma." He puts his arm around her shoulder and turns with her toward the castle. "Come, we will get you bathed and warm and fed. Your room is ready. Everything is ready."

She stops. "But—"

Her father puts a finger to her lips. "No," he says. "My sunshine has returned. We will have time to talk of the past. But first, we must celebrate. It will be a feast unlike any other!" He laughs, looking down at the baby. "A grandson! A miracle!"

As the two of them walk together towards the manor, its stone walls gleam in the setting sun and I can think only of fairytales and every other story that ends far better than I could imagine. The vision fades to black.

Emma surges out of the Sieve's water. She breathes heavily, doesn't speak.

"I will not ask what you have seen," Abram says, standing beside us. "I ask only: Cipher, do you endorse Emma as an initiate of the Blue Tower?"

Of course I do. I am more alive to her beauty and spirit than I have ever been. But I look to her. "Do you still want this?"

Tears streak down her cheeks as she nods.

"Yes," I say, "I endorse her."

"Welcome to the Blue Tower," Abram says, tapping the silver link around Emma's neck with his staff, then removing it. He hands her a thick, grayish blue robe with two stripes on the sleeve. "As you have seen and will see as you rise in our ranks, as Cipher has done, this is where we see our pride and scour it away, no matter what it takes."

# 55

AFTER THE INITIATION, Abram tells me to take Emma to her room, and that I'll know which one it is because it'll be the only door open this late. He tells us to get some rest for the Scouring tomorrow. And he tells me I need to pick my team of twelve by the morning.

"You've earned their respect now," he says, with his hand on my shoulder. "You are ready."

We say goodnight and I escort Emma to her new room. It's near the bottom of the Blue Tower, and it's just like my first room here—a small, plain space with a bed, a desk, and a narrow slit for a window overlooking the sea. The difference is that she got to start with memories intact, instead of at the bottom of the tower, treading water with a blank-slate mind.

Emma and I are too tired to talk long. What we've seen together from her memory doesn't need explanation. I've learned almost as much about her as she's learned about me. It's amazing how much a single, poignant memory can reveal. I tell her briefly what I saw in the Sieve, the picture of my mother, and that Abram suggested she's in the Red Tower. Emma seems to understand when I say that I have to try to rescue my Mom from Red. But I can't bring myself to tell

Emma yet about my wife and my son. There's still too much I don't know. The wound is too fresh. It hurts too much.

As I begin to leave, Emma asks me, "What do you think Abram meant, when he said you are ready?"

Her question makes me think of Daniel, and of my scar. I hold up my hand, showing it to her. "You know how you couldn't heal this?"

"Yes."

"You know the man from the Green Tower, the one who looks like an old mushroom leaning on a stick?"

She laughs. "How could I forget?"

"He noticed my scar," I say, trying to recall the exact words they'd said. "He told Abram that it meant I was the last one—number seven hundred twenty—and that it meant some kind of end was near."

"The end of the Scouring?"

"I think so..." I use a finger to trace over the two crossing lines of the scar again, remembering the symbol that dangled from my wife's necklace. I try to piece together everything I've learned here—from Sarai's words about finding balance among the towers, to others saying I have the most power they've ever seen, to Abram's hint that I need to enter the White Tower. "What if I'm supposed to help each tower, and the people in them? If the numbers in the towers are balanced, with one hundred forty-four each...I'm not sure, but I think, maybe then we could all leave this place."

"Through the White Tower?" Emma asks, studying me.

"I hope so. I don't want to be stuck here forever."

"None of us do."

"So I have to try whatever it takes."

226

"You're going to leave Blue, aren't you?"

I meet her blue eyes, thinking of her past, and of what we've been through together. "You know how, in the Sieve, things turned out better when you returned home?"

She smiles and nods, even as her eyes tear up.

"Sometimes we know we have to take action, but old wounds hold us back, making us afraid. Nothing good happens without courage. Especially when it comes to those we love most."

"Your mother?" she asks.

"If she's here, I have to find her."

"Take me with you to Red."

*Really?* Emma has just joined Blue, and now she's saying she'll leave if I am leaving. I don't deserve it. And she deserves better—Abram said there was more for her here. "You know I can't control what happens in the Scouring."

"I'm not afraid." Emma puts her hand gently on my cheek. "Not anymore, not when it comes to those I love most. I want to come."

"We'll see." Her touch makes my heart thump loudly in my chest. I lean forward and kiss her lightly on the forehead. "Goodnight, Emma."

# 56

BY LUNCH THE next day I have picked my twelve for the Scouring. We sit around a table in the dining hall, fifty feet underwater and surrounded by glass and sea. I watch a huge sea turtle drift by as I eat squid soup. The tentacles sometimes make me gag when they go down, but otherwise it's fine. I've learned to take what I get. I'll probably even miss the soup, and definitely this room, once I'm gone.

The faces at the table are familiar now. Emma, Hank, Helena, Tom, Pierre, Shelley, and the others who had joined us for the Hunting. I decided not to change anything about the group. One of them had been sent back to the beginning, so Emma took his place.

I still haven't figured out exactly how I'm going to handle her request to take her with me to the Red Tower. There must be a way to protect the others if I let myself get caught. They shouldn't have to go down because of me. No one wants to get wiped. No one wants to be a servant of another tower. But for me, I've decided it's worth the risk. My Mom is there. Who knows what Red does to its people—can't be good. She could be trapped. And maybe Red won't wipe me. Abram says I'm different. Daniel, too, and he's probably talked to Red's leaders. They might know about me. Their numbers have been falling. They'll want my power on their side.

So I need a plan. How do I get to Red without making my team take the risk that only I should bear. I've thought of the options, none good. If I'm captured early in the Scouring, our group will scatter and get rounded up. If I'm captured late, we'll probably have already caught someone else while defending our group and the whole Scouring would end. We also can't go to the center of the Scouring or I'll get lost in some memory—too uncertain. So not in the beginning or the end or the center, it must be along the wall, in the rush of things. It's all too unpredictable.

"Cipher, what do you think?" Hank asks.

I gag on a tentacle, surprised at how lost in thought I'd been. "Sorry. About what?"

"Green or Yellow? Boy or girl?" Hank asks.

"He wasn't even listening," Helena says. "I told you. He's been in la-la land ever since his last peek in the Sieve. What did you see?"

I don't answer. I don't know what to say.

"See?" Helena looks around the group. "Maybe you should let me lead. It worked last time. Remember the Green boy? I want to catch that same one we met. Jack's brother, Jones."

"He might not even be there," Tom says, turning to me. "Seriously, Cipher. Who should we try to capture?"

My first thought is of Kiyo, in Black. But I know the chances are slim that she'd be in the Scouring—in the twelve out of hundreds from Black. Maybe Helena is right. She could lure someone from Green while I protect the group and watch Red. Once she brings one in, I draw on Emma's power and give my team a tunnel of air to get back, then I turn back to the Scouring and run for the Red tower. They win, I win.

"Good idea," I say, smiling at Helena. "That boy from Green couldn't keep his eyes off you."

Helena quickly wipes the surprise from her face and meets my smile, like she knows I have some ulterior motive. We've known each other long enough that I can't hide that now. "I'm glad we agree," she says. "We will need you to shield us the whole time."

"That's true," Hank says. "Red can control fire."

"And we already saw that old man from Green disappear," Tom says. "So that's kind of hard to fight against."

I hadn't considered that others in Green might be able to do the same thing, unless it's a special power that only their leader has. "What about Black and Yellow?" I ask.

"You know how we can heal?" Emma says, leaning forward. "Well, the rumor in the Yellow Tower is that the masters of that power can change what people want. By healing, touching someone inside, they can control someone's desire."

"How do we stop that?" Pierre asks.

Emma shrugs. "Don't know."

"And Black?" I ask.

No one answers, and around the table I see only heads shaking, faces filled with fear.

"Black is a mystery," Hank says. "They have weapons, of course, because they have iron. And they tend to stay close

230

together. We should stay away from them. There's gotta be some way they've become so strong."

As our group agrees with this and continues talking strategy, I remember what Daniel and Abram had spoken about—how the Black Tower keeps rising. That makes the towers further from equilibrium. Maybe, after I rescue my Mom, it'll be time to focus on Black. I still wonder what is happening to Kiyo there. I doubt that it's good.

If Red will teach me how to control fire like I control the air…then I'd be ready to take on Black.

# 57

A FEW HOURS later the twelve of us walk together down the tunnel and toward the gate to the Scouring. Abram and Sarai are there, beside the board showing the tally for each tower:

*Black 360*
*Blue 143*
*Red 88*
*Yellow 67*
*Green 62*

The order has changed again. Blue is only one person away from 144—the number each tower needs for equilibrium. Yellow and Green need the most help, but that's not where my mother is.

As the gates lift, we enter the Scouring in a double-file line to the left, along the wall toward Green. I look over our group, seeing Emma, Hank. My throat feels tight so I say the words softly, "Respect the mind."

"Respect the mind," they respond.

Unlike the first time we did this, we know what we're doing. We're focused. We fall quiet, and the color of our robes blends in with the tall gray wall.

Across the vast open space, Black has split up. One half moves to the center, while the other comes straight at us, like we have a target painted on us. They march like a single organism—a phalanx. Legs step in unison, every one of them dressed in the same black. We have twice their number, but as they start running, long spears rise overhead, and we have nowhere to run. They're thirty feet away when they throw their weapons. It looks like a black rushing wave. Someone in our group shouts my name.

I reach for the wind.

But something bats at my power, not shutting it down, but dividing it, weakening it. In the last instant I manage to fling up a shield of air and knock a handful of the weapons to the ground in front of me. I miss the others.

Shouts of pain erupt beside me.

Three of us are down. Tom is writhing on the ground, screaming.

Emma kneels beside him, trying to calm him, heal him.

We don't have time to recover. The rush of figures from Black are on us now. They're clothed head to toe in black, so I can see only their eyes. But that's all I need to see to know that one of them is a boy as big as Hank, hard as iron, locked in on me.

I move too late. He tackles me hard against the stone wall. My shoulder and arm blaze in pain, then feel numb. He pulls out a rope and grabs my wrist. He's going to tie my hands.

*My Mom didn't read my story. She couldn't read it. My father was gone. She was alone, working so hard, trapped. I was alone. I became a wreck of a person.* But now I can save her. Except Black is in my way. All my memories and furies swirl into a storming rage.

233

Black took Kiyo. The Black Tower that never loses…until now.

The wind forms like a fist, grabbing the boy from Black. His eyes open in shock as he lifts off the ground. I fling the air and throw him away, sliding across the stone.

Emma is holding out her hand to me. I take it and stand. All around us the fight spreads. Boys from Black have tied up a few of us already. They're dragging Helena and two others away. Only Hank and Pierre still seem to be free, wrestling against two boys on the ground. A group from Green is approaching to our left.

"Let me have control," Emma says, urgent. "They're focused on you. They won't stop me fast enough."

I don't understand, but I trust her. I grab her hand and pull on my power, imagining myself holding it out in open hands, offering it to her.

Emma seizes control, like she's yanking a thread out of my body. I can see her weaving the threads together—yellow and blue coiling around—and directing them towards our group. She unties every rope and turns them back against Black. Two boys go down, ropes binding their legs, but the other ropes fall harmlessly on the ground. A person from Black, a hooded girl, is pointing at Emma and shouting. Her voice almost sounds familiar.

Three boys from Black charge, and four from Green are coming at us, too. Helena is halfway across the Scouring, being hauled away.

I start to feel trapped, like we are going to be pinned in this spot against the wall while they all surround us and overwhelm us. We cannot hold against them. There's no chance for Helena.

I seize control from Emma, drawing more of her power than ever before. I'm sweating, shaking, as I gather the air and the light to form a wall around us.

*Tie it.* This is Emma's voice, inside my head.

I do what she says, sealing the edges of the shield to the ground, but it won't hold. A barrage of dark lines slams against the wall. Each hit makes the translucent surface crack. The attacks are coming too fast, the cracking spreading before I can fuse them back together.

In desperation I let go of the wall and use all my power to try to grab the dark lines, to control them. But I can't. They're like smoke. The best I can do is follow them to their source— the hooded girl in black.

"Her," I say, pointing, and Emma understands.

We charge at her, while I weave my power against hers. I don't hesitate before I slam into her, both of us tumbling to the ground. Just as I pin her down, I glimpse two boys from black raising their spears at me.

It's now or never. Control this girl's power, or get captured and wiped.

I close my eyes. I remember when I first arrived in the Blue Tower, in the dark water of the cave underneath, where I had to swim ahead, into the unknown, to survive. I do the same now, letting this girl's power flood over me while I hold a dense core of air and light in the center. I feel Emma's power, her memories of her family and her son. I let this new source of power inside, my pulse quickens, my body exhilarated. I have all three powers coursing through me—air, light, and something like molten iron.

My eyes open to see the spears a foot from me in midair. Time moves slowly as I clench my fist and all the power. The spears fall. The boys from Black fall. And I feel all the air in the Scouring in my grip, motionless and defenseless against me. Not a single molecule of oxygen can move. Not even a breath. All the faces around me are stunned. Hands move to throats. Asphyxiating.

There's a small tug on my shirt. It's the girl from Black. Only her eyes are visible through her head-covering, but that's enough for me to know.

"Please," she croaks, breathless. "Save me."

Her eyes swallow me. Narrow, dark as night, with flecks of gold like stars.

"Kiyo."

"Please. Stop."

I let go of all the air at once, like exhaling the deepest breath I could hold.

# 58

KIYO IS WITH me, pulling on my arm and scrambling to her feet. She looks over her shoulder. "They're running," she says. "I'm free…"

Everything has changed since I froze the air in the Scouring. Everyone nearby is running…away from me. A fight has broken out near the Green gate, between Green and Red and Black. I see flashes of fire. My group from Blue has scattered. Two boys from Black are dragging someone away. Her blond hair looks golden against their clothes. Emma.

"Stop them." Kiyo grabs my collar, shaking me. "Cipher, now!"

I pull the air, breathing deep, and form a net. This time nothing tries to interfere with my power. It's as easy as folding paper as my net sweeps under the two boys. I knock them away from Emma and pick them up, like two dark marbles dangling in mid-air.

"Take me with you," Kiyo begs. "Back to Blue."

"Of course."

She smiles faintly, shaking her head. "They said I was destined for Black, but I found you."

A loud shout pulls our attention back to the Scouring. A group from Black is circling back our way, skirmishing with Red at the edges of the white square. "We have to go," Kiyo says. "There's another girl with Black. She's more powerful than I am. She will stop you."

This must be what Kiyo did. I don't have time to ask more now. Instead I take Kiyo's hand and run after Emma. She's backing away from the two boys from Black, still hanging a few feet off the ground, thrashing against my invisible net.

No one gets in my way. When I reach Emma, I take her hand, standing between her and Kiyo. I have to get them back, now.

I try what I did before—drawing on the power of both girls, weaving it into mine. This time I'm not under attack, so I see more of what the spiral of blue, yellow, and black can do. I begin to harden the smoke-like black from Kiyo, forging it into a metal, shaping it like clay in my hands. I mold the metal into a tunnel along the ground between us and the Blue Tower's gate. I manage to safely enclose five from my team, who have made their way to the gate. Once the metal hardens, it takes no more effort to hold it in place. We have a protected path back.

The two boys in Black still dangle in my net. I use the power to make bands of metal around their wrists and ankles, clasped together by chains. Then I pull on the net, dragging them through the air towards the tunnel. Their eyes are terrified and helpless as they pass. I push them all the way to the end of the tunnel, bound by our gate. Maybe I can catch more. Maybe I can capture everyone.

But first I need to secure the rest of my team. They have scattered among the skirmishes nearby. I shout as loud as I can: "Blue, to me! To me! Blue!"

My voice carries easily across the bare stone of the Scouring, echoing off the high walls. Eyes turn to me. More eyes than I wanted.

I begin weaving the three powers together again, but this time there's resistance. A dense, dark cloud begins to form around me, making it almost impossible to see.

*The girl from black*, Kiyo says, through our connection. *Monica.*

The cloud only darkens more. It's like volcanic ash, swirling around me. I try to force my way through, but there's no trace of light left. I feel blind, unable to see beyond Emma, Kiyo, and me.

I squeeze Emma's hand. "Take control."

The moment she grabs the thread of power, I can see perfectly again. People are charging at us from all around, like we're a magnet.

Hank is the closest, pulling along three others from our group, including Tom, Pierre, and Shelley. He's shouting something. "Run! Go back! Run!"

Behind him there's three from Red, charging after him. A ball of flame forms in their midst, then blazes forward.

Emma weaves yellow and blue to drop a wall in front of the fire. An explosion throws us back, the flame blasting against the wall, shattering it like glass.

I stumble to my feet as Hank and the others reach us. "Get in!" I shout, pointing to the tunnel. "It leads back. We'll be right behind you."

Their faces are confused as they pass, but they don't stop or say a word. We duck into the tunnel after them, running as fast as we can towards the Blue gate.

I'm the last one to reach the group by the gate. No one has followed. There are eleven of us here from Blue, plus the two boys and Kiyo from Black. We are missing Helena.

Emma seems unaffected by whatever the girl from Black did, but she also seems unable to use the thread from Kiyo. As the gate opens for us, I tell everyone to get inside quickly.

Then, as soon as everyone has gone through, I take the power from Emma. The smoke has parted slightly, just enough for me to slam the gate shut. It is too heavy for my group to lift from inside, and the only opening is a slit to look through—as wide as the door, but far too narrow to pass through.

Emma's eyes appear in the slit. Then Hank's and Kiyo's beside hers.

"Open it!" Hank shouts from the other side. "Now!"

We do not have long before the Scouring will end. I lean close to them. "I'm sorry, I have to go."

"No!" Hank looks furious. "What are you talking about? You have to come now."

I shake my head. "Take care of Emma and Kiyo, okay?"

Hank is scowling, but he nods.

"You're going to Red," Emma says. "Without us."

She's right. This is my burden. Not theirs. "My Mom is there. She might need help. I'll find her and bring her back."

Hank shouts that it's ridiculous, that I can't go, that Blue needs me.

But Kiyo and Emma are quiet, their questioning eyes

disarming me. I think of their pasts, of Kiyo marching through the snow and losing her son, of Emma living in squalor, losing her husband. Emma manages to slide her slender arm through the narrow slit in the gate. She touches my cheek, and I feel her healing my shoulder and arm. She feels so close.

"I might lose my memories, everything," I say. "I can't let any of you risk that. And somebody has to remind me who I am, right?"

"Respect the mind," Hank says softly.

Emma smiles, tears in her eyes, as she strokes my cheek softly. "I won't forget, Cipher. Neither will you."

I say goodbye and turn back down the tunnel. I can't look back. It hurts more than I could have imagined to leave behind those three sets of eyes. But I'm ready to suffer, to do whatever it takes to reach my mother.

# 59

AS I WALK back through the tunnel, its smooth metallic walls lining the way, my mind turns from the Blue Tower and the friends behind me toward the Red Tower ahead. This is not going to be easy, especially alone.

I stop at the tunnel's opening. Most of the fighting is around the outer edge of the Scouring. There are others from the Black Tower going against Green and Yellow. One of them is probably the girl who Kiyo mentioned, Monica. If she can stop my powers, I doubt I'll make it. Better not to draw any power, to avoid attention. Time to find another way.

The path through the center, over the white circle, is wide open, with the Red Tower looming on the other side. A few people from Red wait near their gate. If I can just get to them... But I remember the last time I set foot on the white circle. I was transported to a memory in a hospital—full of pain and sickness and regret—then the Scouring had ended with booming words and a flash of burning flame. I don't want to repeat that, but I know so much more now. If a memory comes, I'll be ready, no surprises. It's my best option.

I make a run for it, dashing straight toward the middle and the Red gate beyond. I'm at a full sprint when I cross the line of gray stone into the white circle. Two steps later it happens again. Everything shifts.

A hospital hallway lies ahead, with rooms lining both sides. It is the same as before, with fluorescent lights above and sterile floors below. This time, though, I see that there's an open doorway at the end of the hall, still showing the Red Tower in the distance. Must keep going. Ignore what's around. Run.

But near the end of the hallway a familiar voice makes me freeze. It comes from a doorway to my left, so close, so important. I can't help but glance inside the room, where I see what I saw before—five people huddling over a hospital bed. One of them is me, Dr. Fitzroy. Standing across from me is a woman, and this time I know her: my wife. On the bed there's a young boy with a shaved head, my son, looking small and frail and connected to a dozen tubes. The look on my older face shows despair, or worse. I hear myself saying, "This wasn't supposed to happen. I could have saved him. I…"

Suddenly something slams into me, hard as a freight train, knocking me completely out of the hospital and onto the gray stone of the Scouring, the white circle behind me. A boy from Black is pinning me down. He pulls back a fist and lands a punch square on my jaw.

The pain is shattering. I grab desperately for the air, managing to weave just enough to throw the boy back a few feet. I stagger to my feet, head ringing.

Then I'm hit from behind, making me lose grip of the air. It's an older boy from Red with a thick brown beard. He glares at me from a metal helmet with huge horns rising out of its sides. His head is coming at me. Before I even know

243

what he's doing, he headbutts me.

Forehead onto nose. Bones smash. Stars erupt.

Lights blink on and off, dancing around his horns. But the helmeted boy is already off me, spinning to face the one from Black who is coming again. The two of them clash like titans.

Through the stars I remember—must get to Red. I scramble to my knees and grab at the air, my focus fumbling but holding just enough. I flick the boy from Black away. The helmeted boy turns to me, shocked.

This is my chance. I'll tell him I want to join his tower.

"Hey—" I begin, but the smoke from Black is suddenly around me, blocking my power and knocking me back. My foot steps onto the white circle again.

The hospital room looks alive with beeping sounds and monitor lights, but it smells like sterile death. Shame hits me all over. I try to shake it away, to get out of my white coat and out of the room with the sick boy, my son, but the smoke is here, too. I can't see or feel anything else. *I failed. I failed. I...*

Another blow hits me, right in the gut. Then I'm dragged out of the hospital room. Relief floods over me, but doesn't last long.

It's the Scouring.

The boy from Red rears his head back again. I can't even react before his helmeted forehead crashes into me.

More stars. Bones hurt. I collapse in pain.

"Now you'll stay down," the boy mutters, as he grabs my body and hauls it onto his shoulder like a sack of potatoes.

It's not hard to play dead. I let myself sag against him, motionless. I taste iron in my mouth and see blood drop to the ground, trailing behind me. Hanging there, upside down, I see that the boy is heading to the Red Tower on the craggy mountain above. My bloody lips can't help but curl into a painful smile.

I've done it. I've finished treading water. I'm going to my Mom. I'm going to the Red Tower.

Don't miss *The Red Tower*, the sequel to *The Blue Tower* and the second book in The Five Towers Series, available on Amazon and more.

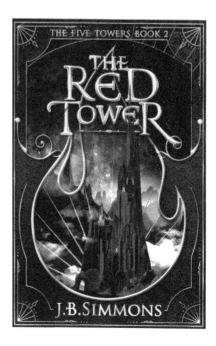

Printed in the USA
CPSIA information can be obtained
at www.ICGtesting.com
LVHW040824151023
761015LV00051B/573